barthpenn@heaven.org

the story of young Jordon Mink
and the email he got from Heaven.

kevin scott collier

Baker Trittin Press
Winona Lake, Indiana

barthpenn@heaven.org
By Kevin Scott Collier

Printed in the United States of America
Cover Art: Thea Collier

Published by Tweener Press Division
Baker Trittin Press
P.O. Box 277
Winona Lake, Indiana 46590

To order additional copies please call (574) 269-6100
or email info@btconcepts.com
http://www.gospelstoryteller.com

Publishers Cataloging-Publication Data
Collier, Kevin Scott
        barthpenn@heaven.org / Kevin Scott Collier - Winona Lake,
        Indiana   Baker Trittin Press, 2004

                p.   cm.

Library of Congress Control Number: 2004113579
ISBN: 0-9752880-2-4
        1. Juvenile   2. Fiction   3. Religious   4. Christian
        I: Title   II. barthpenn@heaven.org
JUV033010

Dedicated
to two Angels on Earth
Corina and Paige Collier

Sunday, May 25, 2003, a young boy named Jordon Mink
received a misdirected email,
a communication not meant for him.
It would not only change his life
but save it as well.

This is his story. . . .

\<Chapter One\>

\<A BREACH IN HEAVEN\>

Subject: You are late!
From: Bartholomew Pennington <barthpenn@heaven.org>
Date: Sun, 25 May 2003 14:31:12
To: jordonmink@intelweb.com

Dear Mr. Mink,

You cannot remain on earth any longer. I urgently request your arrival here in Heaven. You have no idea what a precarious position you have placed me in.

I fully understand our agreement, but due to scheduling commitments on behalf of St. Andrew I shall have to attend to your request at a later date. I realize we have an arrangement, and I shall make good on that request ASAP.

I implore you to be here in Heaven by tomorrow, no later.

We shall talk upon your arrival.

Sincerely,
Bartholomew Pennington
Angel, 2nd Order
Cloud Nine, Heaven

From: Jordon Mink <jordonmink@intelweb.com>
To: barthpenn@heaven.org
Sent: Mon, 26 May 2003 16:12:07
Subject: Hey dude!

Hey BART,

I got your letter. I don't think it was meant for me!!! Have YOU GOT the wrong Jordon Mink??? What gives?!!!

Are you like an angel? Is THIS a joke??? And who's this guy you're supposed to meet? Do you have the Internet up there?

Anyway, F.Y.I. I'm 10 years old and live in Janesville,Wisconsin.

Write again, OK?

g2g,
Jordon

Subject: Security Breach
From: Bartholomew Pennington <barthpenn@heaven.org>
Date: Tues, 27 May 2003 07:47:23
To: st.andrew@kingdom.org

Dearest St. Andrew,

I regret to inform you I may have caused a security breach in Heaven. I need not be reminded of how we were cautioned upon implementation of the new system for communication with our Operatives on Earth.

A Mr. Jordon Mink passed away last Friday and is defiantly keeping his soul on earth pending fulfillment of a promise I made him. I assure you, Mr. Mink will make a fine Angel 3rd Order Apprentice.

Anyway, to make a long story short, I erroneously transmitted a communication to the *wrong* Jordon Mink on Earth. I have received a response from a 10-year-old boy. He now has my email address!

I deeply regret this error and offer my sincerest apologies.

The boy's letter appears below. Please advise ASAP.

Sincerely,
Bartholomew Pennington
Angel, 2nd Order
Cloud Nine, Heaven

>*From: Jordon Mink* <jordonmink@intelweb.com>
>*To: barthpenn@heaven.org*
>*Sent: Mon, 26 May 2003 16:12:07*
>*Subject: Hey dude!*
>
>*Hey BART,*
>
>*I got your letter. I don't think it was meant for me!!! Have YOU*
>*GOT the wrong Jordon Mink??? What gives?!!!*

>
>*Are you like an angel?*
>
>*Is THIS a joke?? And who's this guy you're supposed to meet?*
>*Do you have the Internet up there?*
>
>*Anyway, F.Y.I. I'm 10 years old and live in Janesville,*
>*Wisconsin.*
>
>*Write again, OK?*
>
>*g2g,*
>*Jordon*

Subject: Concerning the breach
From: Andrew Wellsworth III <st.andrew@kingdom.org>
Date: Wed, 28 May 2003 10:18:02
To: barthpenn@heaven.org

Dear Bartholomew,

I cannot stress to you enough how great a concern your error is.
St. Hawthorne is most concerned! It took several blessings just
to calm him!

St. Hawthorne and I have both agreed that we wish to keep this
contained at the moment and not have it reach "the higher ups."

An attachment appears below to send to the boy, Jordon Mink.
Once he opens it the breach should be secure and remedy the
situation immediately. The attachment will erase your email
address not only from the boy's computer but from his mind as
well.

I trust I shall hear no more of this problem.

Sincerely,
St. Andrew
Administrator of Angels, 1ˢᵗ Order
The Kingdom of God

❑   Attachment - Memory Gone

Subject: Questions answered
From: Bartholomew Pennington <barthpenn@heaven.org>
Date: Wed, 28 May 2003 17:37:49
To: jordonmink@intelweb.com

Hello Jordon,

Sorry for the delay getting back to you, but some problems surfaced that required my attention.

Do you want to see something really cool? You can access the website to Heaven by tapping on the little icon below. There you will find the answers to all of your questions!

Enjoy!

Sincerely,
Bartholomew Pennington

❑   Attachment - Memory Gone

Subject: It's a done deal
From: Bartholomew Pennington <barthpenn@heaven.org>
Date: Wed, 28 May 2003 17:50:14
To: st.andrew@kingdom.org

Dearest St. Andrew,

I sent the erasure attachment to the boy, Jordon Mink.

The actual Jordon Mink who passed away arrived here two days ago, and that situation is close to being resolved. He is being oriented in the formalities and responsibilities of Angel 3rd Order, Earth Operative.

I still must fulfill a commitment concerning the performance of a small comfort assurance I pledged to Mr. Mink for his young son, Wesley. I will descend to earth tomorrow to administer that "touch of assurance." It will be elementary but nonetheless effective.

Perhaps, if you're not too busy by week's end, we can rendezvous to catch up and discuss your new position. I recall not too long ago we shared the same cloud before you became my director. Belated congratulations!

Talk to you soon.

Sincerely,
Bartholomew Pennington
Angel, 2nd Order
Cloud Nine, Heaven

barthpenn@heaven.org

From: Jordon Mink <jordonmink@intelweb.com>
To: barthpenn@heaven.org
Sent: Thurs, 29 May 2003 15:45:59
Subject: Hey loser!

Hey BART,

NICE TRY, loser!!! MEMORYGONE? Yeah, RIGHT!! Do you
think I'm stupid?????

I trashed your lame attachment. That was really stupid, DUDE!
A VIRUS ALERT came up, so I knew it was a lie. LIAR!!!! I
thought angels didn't lie!!!

MAYBE I should tell your boss or something. BAD ANGEL,
VERY BAD ANGEL!!!!

I'm not even sure you are an angel. You had better write back
soon and come clean, or I'll forward your letters to everyone I
know!!! AND, that's a fact, Jack!

g2g,
Jordon

Subject: The kid is back
From: Bartholomew Pennington <barthpenn@heaven.org>
Date: Fri, 30 May 2003 0:7:08:13
To: st.andrew@kingdom.org

Dearest St. Andrew,

I regret to inform you the boy I brought to your attention on Tuesday, one Jordon Mink, has returned. He did not open the attachment, and it angered him.

He's threatened to forward my email address to other mortals! Also, he has threatened to inform God Almighty that I tried to deceive him! (Can he do that?)

Perhaps you and I can resolve this and not alarm St. Hawthorne any further?

The young boy's letter appears below.

What must I do? Please advise ASAP.

Sincerely,
Bartholomew Pennington
Angel, 2nd Order
Cloud Nine, Heaven

>*From:* Jordon Mink <jordonmink@intelweb.com>
>*To:* barthpenn@heaven.org
>*Sent:* Thurs, 29 May 2003 15:45:59
>*Subject:* Hey loser!
>
>Hey BART,
>
>NICE TRY, loser!!! MEMORYGONE? Yeah, RIGHT!! Do you
>think I'm stupid?????
>
>I trashed your lame attachment. That was really stupid,
>DUDE! A VIRUS ALERT came up, so I knew it was a lie.
>LIAR!!!! I thought angels didn't lie!!!

>

>MAYBE I should tell your boss or something. BAD ANGEL,
>VERY BAD ANGEL!!!!
>

>I'm not even sure you are an angel. You had better write back
>soon and come clean, or I'll forward your letters to everyone I
>know!!! AND, that's a fact, Jack!
>

>g2g,
>Jordon

Subject: Oh, great!
From: Andrew Wellsworth III <st.andrew@kingdom.org>
Date: Fri, 30 May 2003 09:23:51
To: barthpenn@heaven.org

Dear Bartholomew,

This matter is of grave concern, I assure you. We *cannot*
relinquish the email address of an Angel in Heaven to *any*
mortal! You have placed me in a precarious situation, Brother
Bartholomew, as I was one of the key proponents in
implementing this mortal form of communication to allow our
Earth Operatives to blend in.

Now, we have a breach of Heaven. What is next, Bartholomew?
Will it be kids hacking into our Heavenly Mainframe or *SPAM*?
This is atrocious! You and I may lose our wings over this!

Against my better judgment, perhaps you should just ask the
child what he wants until we further review how to remedy this.
It can't make matters worse. He already possesses a direct line
to Cloud Nine thanks to you!

I implore you to be discrete concerning future communications
with the child. The less he knows the better. I will be
in touch. *Count on it!*

Sincerely,
St. Andrew
Administrator of Angels, 1ˢᵗ Order
The Kingdom of God

P.S. Can Jordon tell God you lied to him? Surely you jest.
Through prayer, Jordon can, indeed, "tell on you!" You caused
this mess. Now fix it!

From: Jordon Mink <jordonmink@intelweb.com>
To: barthpenn@heaven.org
Sent: Fri, 30 May 2003 16:47:12
Subject: I'm WAITING!!!

Hey BART,

I'm putting my hands together. I'm gonna tell YOU KNOW WHO you're a LIAR!!! I'm getting ready to forward your emails to like everyone on the PLANET!!!!

Are YOU SWEATIN your HALO OFF YET???? LOL

You'd best cough up the facts, Jack, or you're toast!

g2g,
Jordon

Subject: Hello again!
From: Bartholomew Pennington <barthpenn@heaven.org>
Date: Fri, 30 May 2003 17:02:13
To: jordonmink@intelweb.com

Hello Jordon,

Sorry for my delay in responding, but things have been, well, kind of busy up here. I apologize for deceiving you, but I am *in fact* an Angel.

I would appreciate it very much if you wouldn't forward my email address or correspondence with you to others. Perhaps, Jordon, we can strike a bargain in good faith.

I will agree to become your pen pal if you promise to delete every letter I send after you have read it and promise to tell no one of our friendship. To be frank, I may lose my wings over this and be reassigned as an Earth Operative chasing down Satan's evil imps. I have worked hard to achieve a position here on Cloud Nine. If I were ordered to relinquish this position, our correspondence would cease in an instant.

If you can help me, Jordon, I surely can help you. Please allow me another chance.

Can we trust each other?

Sincerely,
Bartholomew Pennington
Angel, 2nd Order
Cloud Nine, Heaven

P.S. – What does g2g mean?

From: Jordon Mink <jordonmink@intelweb.com>
To: barthpenn@heaven.org
Sent: Sat, 31 May 2003 08:31:36
Subject: It's cool

Hey BART,

I'm cool with that, so don't SPAZ OUT, OK? I'll trash all the emails and keep my mouth shut.

I'd like to learn about what it's like up there, but I gotta get packed. I won't be able to get back to you until Monday. I have a family picnic to go to . . . you know, hot dogs and hamburgers and stuff. Mmmmmmmmmmmm! GR-8! LOL. We will be camping out too!

My sister is already whining about what to wear. DUH!!!!! It's a trip not a fashion show!

Sorry if I got you in trouble, but don't lie to me any more. Got it?

g2g,
Jordon

P.S. g2g = got to go. OK?

Subject: Situation appears under control
From: Bartholomew Pennington <barthpenn@heaven.org>
Date: Sun, 01 June 2003 12:03:16
To: st.andrew@kingdom.org

Dearest St. Andrew,

For your information, the situation involving the boy, Jordon Mink, is being managed. I hope the kid keeps his promise. He sounds sincere, but we both know how kids can behave!

Perhaps, St. Andrew, we can arrange that rendezvous I mentioned last week for this week.

Again, you have my deepest apologies regarding this situation.

Sincerely,
Bartholomew Pennington
Angel, 2nd Order
Cloud Nine, Heaven

The boy's letter...

>*From: Jordon Mink* <jordonmink@intelweb.com>
>*To: barthpenn@heaven.org*
>*Sent: Sat., 31 May 2003 08:31:36*
>*Subject: It's cool*
>
>*Hey BART,*
>
>*I'm cool with that, so don't SPAZ OUT, OK? I'll trash all the*
>*emails and keep my mouth shut.*
>
>*I'd like to learn about what it's like up there, but I gotta get*
>*packed. I won't be able to get back to you until Monday. I have*
>*a family picnic to go to . . . you know, hot dogs and hamburgers*
>*and stuff. Mmmmmmmmmmmm! GR-8! LOL. We will be*
>*camping out too!*
>
>*My sister is already whining about what to wear. DUH!!!!!! It's*

>
>*a trip not a fashion show!*
>
>*Sorry I got you in trouble, but don't lie to me anymore. Got it?*
>
>*g2g.*
>*Jordon*
>
>*P.S. g2g = got to go. OK?*

Subject: Concerning young Jordon Mink
From: Andrew Wellsworth III <st.andrew@kingdom.org>
Date: Mon, 02 June 2003 07:34:41
To: barthpenn@heaven.org

Dear Bartholomew,

I took it upon myself to contact our Earth Operative, Daniel
Hillsdale, who navigates the territory near Janesville,
Wisconsin. I asked him to check the youth, Jordon Mink. Angel
3rd Order Hillsdale has observed Jordon Mink and his family
and uncovered some news I am sorry to bring to your attention.

Jordon Mink has a terminal illness and will succumb to it in as
little as two months. Neither the boy nor his parents will be
aware of this until the lad begins to show first signs of illness. I
wish I could offer more information, but we cannot foresee all
mortal events.

Due to these circumstances, Brother Bartholomew, tread
delicately when corresponding with him. Do not say anything
that may anger him which could provoke him to relinquish your
email address or forward your mail to others. He will be passing
our way soon, and when he does, Angel 3rd Order Hillsdale will
be directed to erase any remnants of your emails from the
child's computer. Brother Hillsdale will be kept out of the loop
until those services are required.

So, concerning your new pen pal, entertain him, amuse him, but
whatever you do, do not become emotionally attached or
relinquish any secrets of Heaven.

In a very short time this problem will be resolved.

Sincerely,
St. Andrew
Administrator of Angels, 1st Order
The Kingdom of God

Subject: Re: Concerning young Jordon Mink
From: Bartholomew Pennington <barthpenn@heaven.org>
Date: Mon, 02 June 2003 12:48:51
To: st.andrew@kingdom.org

Dearest St. Andrew,

Understood.

Sincerely,
Bartholomew Pennington
Angel, 2nd Order
Cloud Nine, Heaven

Subject: Request profile on Jordon Mink
From: Bartholomew Pennington <barthpenn@heaven.org>
Date: Mon, 02 June 2003 13:01:22
To: danhillsdale@heaven.org

Dear Daniel,

St. Andrew has informed me of your observance of one ten-year-old Jordon Mink who resides in Janesville, Wisconsin.

If you could please afford me your time, would you follow the boy, Jordon Mink, observe his environment, and report a profile of him to me. I cannot disclose why.

May I also ask you to be discrete and not inform St. Andrew of this request? I understand your desire to be reassigned up here, and I could pull some strings to hasten your arrival.

Thank you,
Bartholomew Pennington
Angel, 2nd Order
Cloud Nine, Heaven

P.S. If you happen upon the city of Beloit, could you please let me know if an ice cream establishment by the name of Mingott's is still in existence? I used to have relatives in that area when I was a child, and our family always made a point to stop there. They had the best hot fudge sundaes on Earth. Not that it matters anymore, just curious!

From: Jordon Mink <jordonmink@intelweb.com>
To: barthpenn@heaven.org
Sent: Mon, 02 June 2003 18:52:13
Subject: Hey dude!

Hey BART,

What's new? I hafta tell you I had the BEST time this weekend camping! My dad put the boat in the lake and took me, mom, and my sister for a spin. I ate too many dogs before the ride and barfed over the side!

SUMMER is my favorite time of year. School ends in a week and THAT is AWESOME!!! I don't like going there anymore!!

Guess what I picked up and played with, dude? A PAINTED turtle! And the paint DIDN'T rub off on my shirt! GET IT????? It's a joke!!!! DUH!!!!!

Hey, do you have turtles in heaven????

Hope you're not in trouble anymore. Really sorry if it was my fault. But at least we became friends, right? That's very cool. WAAAAAAAY COOOOOOL!

g2g ttyl,
Jordon

P.S. Can you see me from up there?

Subject: Painted turtles
From: Bartholomew Pennington <barthpenn@heaven.org>
Date: Tues, 03 June 2003 07:02:17
To: jordonmink@intelweb.com

Hello Jordon,

Sounds as though you had a winning weekend. A painted turtle? What color was it painted? (You see I have a sense of humor too.)

When I was your age, my parents owned a boat on a small lake in Michigan. I learned how to water-ski. I must confess there are times when I miss all those mortal things.

You asked if there are turtles in Heaven. I'm going to keep that one a secret. The answer to your question can be found in the Good Book, Jordon.

I must assume you have homework, so I shall say farewell until our next correspondence.

Sincerely,
Bartholomew Pennington
Angel, 2nd Order
Cloud Nine, Heaven

P.S. What does "ttyl" mean?

Subject: Profile on Jordon Mink
From: Daniel Hillsdale <danhillsdale@heaven.org>
Date: Tues, 03 June 2003 09:27:19
To: barthpenn@heaven.org

Dear Bartholomew,

I was able to spend part of yesterday afternoon shadowing
Jordon Mink as requested. I observed him at his school then
later inside the Mink family residence. You'd like this kid,
Bartholomew. He's got spunk. Here's the rundown on Jordon.

At school, he is virtually ignored by others except for a few
bullies who grant him attention he'd rather not receive. (I
jotted down the names of those little troublemakers and will
check on them later!)

Jordon lives in a small one-story white house in a peaceful
neighborhood in Janesville. His father, Paul, is an insurance
salesman. His mother, Joyce, works part-time at the public
library. He has one sibling, a sister, named Erin. Jordon's
parents are both actively involved in their children's lives.

I snooped around Jordon's room and discovered he plays soccer.
A photo of his team hangs on the wall above a dresser. He is
almost blocked out in the picture because he is standing behind
two taller boys. I didn't find any other photos of youths which
might be considered to be Jordon's friends.

Jordon must be an artist as I observed many drawings of
dinosaurs scattered about his room. There is a computer on a
little desk in one corner. There is also a Bible on his night stand
which curiously has feathers used as bookmarks.

The most interesting discovery was a small diary concealed
under his mattress. It reveals the most about the boy. He has a
very low opinion of himself and never thinks he is good enough
in many endeavors. At times, he even asks himself in writing,
"Why am I such a loser?" His diary is riddled with questions he
asks himself which go unanswered. One page of the diary was

blank. Friday, May 30th. There were other trivial things, if you wish to inquire further.

Glad to be of help,
Daniel Hillsdale
3rd Order Angel, Apprentice
Earth Operative, Wisconsin USA

P.S. Mingott's is still in existence. I took a break there seated next to two rather large women at an outdoor picnic table. Both were consuming huge hot fudge sundaes. They looked quite exquisite . . . the sundaes, that is.

Subject: Thank you
From: Bartholomew Pennington <barthpenn@heaven.org>
Date: Tues, 03 June 2003 10:02:34
To: danhillsdale@heaven.org

Dear Daniel,

I appreciate your assistance. There will be nothing further at this time.

Sincerely,
Bartholomew Pennington
Angel, 2nd Order
Cloud Nine, Heaven

Subject: I am troubled
From: Bartholomew Pennington <barthpenn@heaven.org>
Date: Tues, 03 June 2003 11:24:52
To: genwillow@kingdom.org

Dearest Genny,

I need to talk.

Please do not remind me of how long it has been since my last correspondence.

I have opened a Pandora 's Box in Heaven. I accidentally emailed a mortal on earth. St. Andrew is aware of this, and to a degree, St. Hawthorne too. Initially, the individual, a ten-year-old boy, threatened to relinquish my email address to other mortals.

Shortly thereafter, St. Andrew informed me that an Angel 3rd Order Earth Operative discovered the boy would succumb to a fatal illness and pass our way soon. But, until the boy expires, St. Andrew reluctantly has suggested I continue to correspond with the boy. After this dilemma is over, all traces of our communication will be erased as if it had never occurred.

The boy has promised to keep this a secret from everyone. It seems all he really wants is for me to be his pen pal. Genny, I fear I am growing fond of him. What must I do?

Sincerely,
Bartholomew Pennington
Angel, 2nd Order
Cloud Nine, Heaven

Subject: Here we go again
From: Gennif Willow <genwillow@kingdom.org>
Date: Tues, 03 June 2003 14:21:03
To: barthpenn@heaven.org

Dear Bartholomew,

Never just a social call, is it? Except for having wings, you have changed little since we grew up as friends on Earth.

So this is where I am summoned to "remind you" the scope of the responsibilities for Angel, 2nd Order? A true friend will tell you the truth. Angels, who only tell you what you want to hear, do you no favors.

I will not lecture you in regards to your shenanigans up here, but I offer you this. Angel 3rd Order Earth Operatives are the mortal social workers, Bartholomew, not us. We are assigned above those duties. Your position here involves working with the Earth Operatives and consulting with your Director, St. Andrew. We are not to meddle with mortals but to oversee the harvest that brings them here.

I would not be surprised if you have already directed an Earth Operative to snoop on this boy. The problem with digging holes, Bartholomew, is the deeper you dig the harder it is to get out.

I would suggest you not become emotionally connected to this "pen pal" of yours! We all have work to do up here. Best remember what your real responsibilities are. Just the same, I love you, you rascal. Just watch your tail feathers!

Sincerely,
Gennif Willow
Angel, 2nd Order, Administrative
Cloud 27, Heaven

Subject: Re: Here we go again
From: Bartholomew Pennington <barthpenn@heaven.org>
Date: Tues, 03 June 2003 17:11:41
To: genwillow@kingdom.org

Dearest Genny,

That sure sounded like a lecture to me!

I recall back in Grover's Field when we were kids I actually dug a hole that I could not get out of. If I recall, it was you who ran home to get a rope and rescued me.

I shall be cautious and not be too meddlesome concerning the boy.

Sincerely,
Bartholomew Pennington
Angel, 2nd Order
Cloud Nine, Heaven

Subject: Digging holes
From: Gennif Willow <genwillow@kingdom.org>
Date: Tues, 03 June 2003 19:22:17
To: barthpenn@heaven.org

Dear Bartholomew,

I remind you this time the expression "digging a hole" is used figuratively.

Best be cautious. There will be no rescue coming from me this time. It's out of my hands.

Sincerely,
Gennif Willow
Angel, 2nd Order, Administrative
Cloud 27, Heaven

From: Jordon Mink <jordonmink@intelweb.com>
To: barthpenn@heaven.org
Sent: Wed, 04 June 2003 16:45:18
Subject: Soccer

Hey BART,

I want to quit my soccer team! I HATE IT!!! We play the
BELOIT BADGERS this Saturday at 9 in the morning, and
they're brutal!!! COOPER MILLIGAN is on their team, and he
always pushes me down. I call him POOPER MILLIGAN. He's a
total loser!!!! He makes fun of me EVERY game.

Why does GOD create evil people???

Coach Jeff just says to DEAL WITH IT!!! Even my teammates
don't like me anymore!!! OH, WELL.

What's UP with you, I mean, besides the clouds? LOL

Tomorrow my class is going on a Field Trip to Chicago to see a
museum. Dad says they got dinosaur skeletons there.
AWESOME!!!!

I'd ask if there are dinosaurs up in Heaven, but I figure you
won't say! I bet if there were dinosaurs in Heaven that they'd
have wings and look like dragons instead! THAT would be
VERY COOL!!!

g2g ttyl,
Jordon

P.S. ttyl=talk to you later

Subject: Soccer and bullies
From: Bartholomew Pennington <barthpenn@heaven.org>
Date: Wed, 04 June 2003 17:04:27
To: jordonmink@intelweb.com

Hello Jordon,

Sorry about the displays of bad behavior at your soccer games. But, Coach Jeff is right when he suggests to "deal with it." Bullies are really not angry with you. They are unhappy with themselves.

God does not create evil people. It is life's influences and our choices which will determine what we shall become. Just remember to be a good influence for others always. We should never wish to become what we despise most.

Have fun in Chicago. I believe you and your classmates will be visiting The Museum of Science and Industry which is fascinating. When I was your age, I went there once. I was most taken by the large replica of a human heart which had passageways you could walk through. It made me imagine if mortals could see into each other's hearts, the troubles on Earth could be resolved.

Nice hearing from you. Have fun.

Sincerely,
Bartholomew Pennington
Angel, 2nd Order
Cloud Nine, Heaven

From: Jordon Mink <jordonmink@intelweb.com>
To: barthpenn@heaven.org
Sent: Thurs, 05 June 2003 20:32:06
Subject: Drop dead, LOSER!

Hey LOSER,

DEAL WITH IT????? That's all I ever hear from people!

DEEEAAAAALLLLL WITH IT!!!!

Easy for you to say sitting on some cloud up there!!! I thought
YOU would understand. BUT NO!!! I saw the BIG HEART at
the museum in Chicago. TOO BAD you don't have a BIG
HEART yourself!

Coach Jeff will make a GOOD Angel some day. You TWO would
get along QUITE well!!!

HEY, don't write me anymore. OK?

bye,
Jordon

\<Chapter Two\>

\<DOWNLOADING\>

Subject: It's me again
From: Bartholomew Pennington <barthpenn@heaven.org >
Date: Fri, 06 June 2003 07:01:11
To: genwillow@kingdom.org

Dearest Genny,

I am troubled. Jordon emailed me this:

>*From: Jordon Mink* <jordonmink@intelweb.com>
>*To: barthpenn@heaven.org*
>*Sent: Thurs, 05 June 2003 20:32:06*
>*Subject: Drop dead, LOSER!*
>
>*Hey LOSER,*
>
>*DEAL WITH IT????? That's all I ever hear from people!*
>
>*DEEEAAAALLLLL WITH IT!!!!*
>
>*Easy for you to say sitting on some cloud up there!!! I thought YOU would understand. BUT NO!!! I saw the BIG HEART at the museum in Chicago. TOO BAD you don't have a BIG HEART yourself!*
>
>*Coach Jeff will make a GOOD Angel some day. You TWO would get along QUITE well!!!*
>
>*HEY, don't write me anymore. OK?*
>
>*bye,*
>*Jordon*

I simply repeated the advice of his soccer Coach concerning bullies on an opposing team. The Coach had suggested that Jordon should "deal with it." Was this bad advice?

I'm concerned with Jordon being angry with me as he may reveal our rather unusual pen pal relationship with other mortals. I do not wish to bring this to St. Andrew's attention. What must I do?

Sincerely,
Bartholomew Pennington
Angel, 2nd Order
Cloud Nine, Heaven

Subject: Advice?
From: Gennif Willow <genwillow@kingdom.org>
Date: Fri, 06 June 2003 08:31:12
To: barthpenn@heaven.org

Dear Bartholomew,

"Deal with it!"

Sincerely,
Gennif Willow
Angel, 2nd Order, Administrative
Cloud 27, Heaven

Subject: Request your assistance
From: Bartholomew Pennington <barthpenn@heaven.org >
Date: Fri, 06 June 2003 09:21:51
To: danhillsdale@heaven.org

Dear Daniel,

I have an appointment Saturday morning and make a request for your assistance. Would you be so kind as to cover my position here on Cloud Nine between 9:00-11:00 tomorrow? I assure you your absence from Earth will go unreported.

I would prefer this remain in confidence.

Sincerely,
Bartholomew Pennington
Angel, 2nd Order
Cloud Nine, Heaven

Subject: Re: Request your assistance
From: Daniel Hillsdale <danhillsdale@heaven.org>
Date: Fri, 06 June 2003 09:47:04
To: barthpenn@heaven.org

Dear Bartholomew,

Mum's the word. I will arrive on Cloud Nine tomorrow morning to cover for you.

Perhaps when promotions are in order, you could put in a good word on my behalf to St. Andrew? Perhaps for *full* Angel, 3rd Order, or if I may be so ambitious, Angel 2nd Order?

Sincerely,
Daniel Hillsdale
3rd Order Angel, Apprentice
Earth Operative, Wisconsin USA

Subject: Re: Request your assistance
From: Bartholomew Pennington <barthpenn@heaven.org>
Date: Fri, 06 June 2003 12:17:45
To: danhillsdale@heaven.org

Dear Daniel,

Thank you.

Regarding me "putting in a good word" for you with St. Andrew, I'll deal with that later.

Sincerely,
Bartholomew Pennington
Angel, 2nd Order
Cloud Nine, Heaven

From: Jordon Mink <jordonmink@intelweb.com>
To: barthpenn@heaven.org
Sent: Sat, 07 June 2003 14:05:22
Subject: YEAH, it's me!

Hey BART,

I know I said I'd never write you again, but it's killing me!!!!

GUESSSSSSSS WHAAAAAAAT?????? WE WON!!!!

My team won our soccer game and GUESSSSSSSS
WHAAAAAAAT also???
I RULED!!!!!!

POOPER Milligan was calling me names and chasing me, and
just when he tried to trip me flat on my face SOMETHING
tripped him!!! POOPER went down HARD right onto the turf!!!
LOL

LOOOOOOOSER!!!!

Then, when I came up to the goal to score, the Beloit Badger
goalie goes flying off sideways and I SCORE!!!!!! MUST I say IT
WAS the WINNING point????

I wish you could have been there to see me BART!!!
I was AWESOME!!!

I wanted to attach some pictures my dad took of the game, but
he says none of them turned out! There were WHITE STREAKS
all over them! Dad's new digital camera wasn't working right so
he's taking it back to the store tomorrow. What a piece of junk!!!

I HAD to tell you about my winning game! I DEALT WITH IT
and I won! It's kinda nice being a WINNER for ONCE!!!!

But, for the record, I'm still MAD at YOU. OK?

I'm going to Grandma's apartment tomorrow. All next week I have final tests and papers to turn in. SCHOOL is almost OVER. Then it's on to summer!!!

g2g ttyl,
Jordon

Subject: Congratulations!
From: Bartholomew Pennington <barthpenn@heaven.org>
Date: Sat, 07 June 2003 18:31:12
To: jordonmink@intelweb.com

Dear Jordon,

Congratulations on your victory! It sounds like you delivered a stellar performance. I am proud of you, Jordon! I imagine word of this will be the buzz around school on Monday!

Have fun at your Grandmother's place, and good luck with your tests and final assignments. Get back to me when you have the time.

Sincerely,
Bartholomew Pennington
Angel, 2nd Order
Cloud Nine, Heaven

Subject: Digging deeper holes?
From: Gennif Willow <genwillow@kingdom.org>
Date: Sun, 08 June 2003 09:26:57
To: barthpenn@heaven.org

Dearest Bartholomew,

I stopped by Cloud Nine to pay you a visit yesterday morning. I was concerned for you. It was curious to find Daniel Hillsdale (3rd Order Angel, Apprentice) *covering* for you!

You wouldn't by chance have been at a *boy's soccer game* yesterday?

Don't get involved, Bartholomew!

Sincerely,
Gennif Willow
Angel, 2nd Order, Administrative
Cloud 27, Heaven

Subject: Re: Digging deeper holes?
From: Bartholomew Pennington <barthpenn@heaven.org>
Date: Sun, 08 June 2003 14:39:02
To: genwillow@kingdom.org

Dearest Genny,

Do you recall when we were growing up how we used to climb
that old tree near Hunter's Creek so no one would find us?
Then, we would become quiet so we could observe all of God's
tiny creatures around us.

We believed if we remained silent and made not a move that we
would see wonderful things on the ground below. But, at times,
predators lurked in the shadows and innocents stood as prey.
Sometimes we rushed down the tree to disrupt something we
could not bear to see, thus disturbing the cycle of things as they
are.

On Earth, as it is in Heaven, Genny.

More than my soul arrived here in Heaven. My heart did too.

Sincerely,
Bartholomew Pennington
Angel, 2nd Order
Cloud Nine, Heaven

From: Jordon Mink <jordonmink@intelweb.com>
To: barthpenn@heaven.org
Sent: Wed, 11 June 2003 15:41:10
Subject: 1/2 days now

Hey BART,

My tests are all done and papers are all IN. Today was the last full day of school. Tomorrow and Friday are half days and we just hang around and do nothing.

BORRRRRING!!!!

Dad has been talking about sending me to CAMP for a week this summer. HE thinks I'm too quiet and that this will be good for me. YEAH, right! I HATE IT!!! My friend, Peter, says camps are bully breeding grounds. My cousin says it's like being in the Marines!!! I wish Mom and Dad would send my SISTER away instead!!!

I sorta got a job for summer too. It's nothing BIG, but it will get me some $$$. I mow an old man's lawn. He is a VERY strange man!! Mom said he has old timer's disease or something like that. I've done chores for him before, and he never remembers my name! I've told him like a billion times!!! What gives?

I just can't wait to get OUT of school and start enjoying summer.

g2g ttyl,
Jordon

Subject: Going to camp
From: Bartholomew Pennington <barthpenn@heaven.org>
Date: Wed, 11 June 2003 19:47:12
To: jordonmink@intelweb.com

Dear Jordon,

When I was your age, I often did not wish to try anything new. My father, like yours, began planning my journey to a boy's camp one summer and I was aghast! I didn't want to go at all.

I imagined I would likely have to share a cabin with the worst kids there, and they would do everything in their power to humiliate me. I imagined that there would be grand athletic events where captains would pick their teams, and I would be the last boy chosen. I even imagined my parents had sent me there because they wanted to get rid of me.

My father had a saying he repeated often when I didn't want to go somewhere new. He would say, "You're going to have fun whether you like it or not!" I thought that was a silly thing to say. How can anyone have fun whether it is an enjoyable experience or not?

Well, my father was right. In every case, there were peaks and valleys, but I always had fun. And, these experiences always added something to my character.

Let me know how you did on your tests!

Sincerely,
Bartholomew Pennington
Angel, 2nd Order
Cloud Nine, Heaven

From: Jordon Mink <jordonmink@intelweb.com>
To: barthpenn@heaven.org
Sent: Thurs, 12 June 2003 18:41:10
Subject: Mowing lawn

Hey BART,

I mowed the strange old man's lawn this afternoon. There's a lady who lives there, too, but she's NOT his wife. She invited me in for lemonade. It was very HOT outside.

Their house has lots of clocks in it. TICK TICK TICK! The lady introduced herself, but I forget her name. I took a break in the living room with that old man. He just sat there and stared. I have no clue what he was looking at. It was like he wasn't really looking at anything at all!! I talked to him, but he didn't even look at me. It was like I wasn't even there. He's like TOTALLY clueless.

Dad and Mom had brochures out during dinner tonight for Camp Broken Arrow which is about 50 miles from here. I know what they're doing!!!! They're flashing them around to PREPARE ME!!! They have already decided this!!! I know it! I don't want to go to that dump!

Tonight I'm going to Peter's house to play basketball a while.

g2g ttyl,
Jordon

Subject: Don't judge
From: Bartholomew Pennington <barthpenn@heaven.org >
Date: Thurs, 12 June 2003 20:10:32
To: jordonmink@intelweb.com

Dear Jordon,

You really should get to know your neighbors better. This old
gentleman I trust has a name, or is he just the designated
weirdo of the neighborhood? Don't be so quick to judge others
until you really get to know them.

I have heard of Camp Broken Arrow, and there are many things
to do there. Just go with the flow, Jordon. Loosen up. I know
what you fear. You fear connecting with others. True?

Sincerely,
Bartholomew Pennington
Angel, 2nd Order
Cloud Nine, Heaven

From: Jordon Mink <jordonmink@intelweb.com>
To: barthpenn@heaven.org
Sent: Thurs, 12 June 2003 20:21:11
Subject: Butt out!!!

Hey BART,

ARE YOU TRYING TO MAKE ME MAD AGAIN???

I don't need anyone's ADVICE. OK???? Like don't you have some clouds to DUST OFF or something???

g2g,
Jordon

Subject: Sure...
From: Barthpenn@heaven.org <barthpenn@heaven.org>
Date: Thurs, 12 June 2003 20:30:27
To: jordonmink@intelweb.com

Dear Jordon,

I do not "dust."

Sincerely,
Bartholomew Pennington
Angel, 2nd Order
Cloud Nine, Heaven

From: Jordon Mink <jordonmink@intelweb.com>
To: barthpenn@heaven.org
Sent: Fri, 13 June 2003 16:07:51
Subject: I'm DOOMED!!!!

Hey BART,

It's official. I was told I HAVE TO go to summer camp. AND, it's not for ONE week, it's FOR TWO WEEKS!!!!!

I am DOOMED!!!!

I WILL NEVER SURVIVE THIS!!!!

My loser sister is DELIGHTED over the news. I felt like wiping that stupid grin off her freckled face.

Camp Broken Arrow is 50 miles from home, and Dad's bringing me there on June 21st. It's my WORST nightmare.

I got an "A" in every class final! I studied hard this year!! I read over 90 books too!

The old man's NAME is Mr. Baxter. Mom knows him somehow. She says the lady living there is his daughter. You'd think a lady older than Mom would be out living on her own BY NOW!!!

We are going camping this weekend at Crystal Channel. I like swimming in the channel.

Can I ask you a PERSONAL question? HOW did you die?

g2g ttyl,
Jordon

Subject: Have a nice weekend
From: Bartholomew Pennington <barthpenn@heaven.org>
Date: Fri, 13 June 2003 18:42:19
To: jordonmink@intelweb.com

Dear Jordon,

Mr. Baxter, huh? I recall meeting him once in a bookstore.

Don't worry about going to camp. Perhaps Camp Broken Arrow has a computer guests can use to write home. You could write me, but I won't be able to write you while you are at the camp.

How did I die? It doesn't matter, Jordon. It's not how you died; it's how you lived.

Have fun this weekend.

Sincerely,
Bartholomew Pennington
Angel, 2nd Order
Cloud Nine, Heaven

<Chapter Three>

<THE ATTACHMENT>

From: Jordon Mink <jordonmink@intelweb.com>
To: barthpenn@heaven.org
Sent: Sun, 15 June 2003 20:10:36
Subject: I caught a snake!

Hey BART,

Guess what, dude? I caught a snake at Crystal Channel over the weekend! I tossed it at my sister! She screamed like a SPAZ! Hahahahahahahahaha!!!

It was really warm out Saturday. We set up camp right by the channel. I went swimming in the channel most of the day. I found a BIG log to float on and imagined it was a killer whale. I rode on its back and I wrestled it. Guess who WON???

I watched the stars at night. I sneaked out of my tent and climbed a huge willow tree. I sat on a big branch for over an hour in the moonlight. I was staring at the sky looking for Cloud Nine. I was looking for YOU.

I started to get a bit silly!!! I imagined YOU were my Guardian Angel. I imagined you would watch over me and protect me. Yeah, RIGHT! LOL.

I gotta cut Mr. Baxter's lawn tomorrow. That daughter of his must be a REAL slacker or something living off an old man who don't even know what planet he's on!!! It's pretty weird, let me tell you!!!

g2g ttyl,
Jordon

Subject: Guardian Angel?
From: Bartholomew Pennington <barthpenn@heaven.org>
Date: Sun, 15 June 2003 20:37:11
To: jordonmink@intelweb.com

Dear Jordon,

Up here only Saints can assign Guardian Angels to mortals. I regret to inform you that no one here has assigned me to you! However, it would be an honor to be *considered* your Guardian Angel.

You are such a smart young man. You should know where the planet Venus is positioned now in the night sky. If you see two dim tiny stars above it, Cloud Nine is in that area. Unlike the clouds you see on Earth, Cloud Nine is not visible to the naked eye. You will not see it. It is a spiritual place like all of the other clouds that connect the Heavens.

Concerning Mr. Baxter and his daughter: What did I tell you about judging others?

Also, PLEASE use caution when wrestling those killer whales. OK?

Sincerely,
Bartholomew Pennington
Angel, 2nd Order
Cloud Nine, Heaven

From: Jordon Mink <jordonmink@intelweb.com>
To: barthpenn@heaven.org
Sent: Mon, 16 June 2003 18:31:53
Subject: Mr. Baxter

Hey BART,

After I mowed Mr. Baxter's lawn, his daughter invited me in for lemonade again. It's quite tasty!!! Her name is Mrs. Findley, and she's REALLY nice.

My Mom told me Mr. Baxter has ALZHEIMER'S DISEASE (I looked it up.) HE used to be a schoolteacher! Can you imagine? It turns out he was my Mom's 5th grade schoolteacher!!!

This man once knew everything, and now he knows NOTHING???

Mr. Baxter will NEVER be able to teach anyone anything ever again.

BART, why do BAD things happen to GOOD people? Folks like POOPER Milligan just go on forever, and nothing bad ever happens to them!

g2g ttyl,
Jordon

Subject: Re: Mr. Baxter
From: Bartholomew Pennington <barthpenn@heaven.org>
Date: Mon, 16 June 2003 19:02:49
To: jordonmink@intelweb.com

Dear Jordon,

Mr. Baxter's final journey as a mortal is, indeed, sad for those around him. But I disagree with your assertion that he "will never teach anyone anything ever again."

He taught you something important this week. Did he not? This experience will change the way you approach people like him. You will do it with understanding and compassion.

Soon, Mr. Baxter will arrive here, and all that he once knew will return to him. This is his final "lesson" as a human.

Bad things don't *only* happen to good people. It just seems that way. Bad things are unwelcome challenges, disruptive and unsettling, and can even threaten to break our resolve. But winners never give up, Jordon. Winners are resilient. We grieve, heal, learn, and rise above all to become better people. Some of the most compassionate people on Earth today are covered with scars you will never see.

I encourage you to visit with Mr. Baxter every time you mow his lawn, and *even when you don't!* You will not learn anything about *him*, but that is where you will learn a lot about *yourself*.

Sincerely,
Bartholomew Pennington
Angel, 2nd Order
Cloud Nine, Heaven

From: Jordon Mink <jordonmink@intelweb.com>
To: barthpenn@heaven.org
Sent: Tues, 17 June 2003 17:55:02
Subject: I visited Mr. Baxter

Hey BART,

I went over to Mr. Baxter's house today. Mrs. Findley invited me in. I told her I came to pay Mr. Baxter a visit. She was very pleased. She brought me into the living room, and there he was sitting in a chair staring at NOTHING!!!

I took a chair beside him. THEN, I just about FREAKED!!! Mrs. Findley said, "Dad, Jordon Mink has come to visit you." Then, she left the room!!!

It was REALLY WEIRD. I didn't know what to say. I was kinda scared. He coughed and I jumped! His eyes were kinda watery, and he kept blinking, so I got a Kleenex and wiped under his eyes. He still didn't look at me!!!

After a while, I started looking at him and tried to IMAGINE what kind of schoolteacher he once was. That's WHEN I SPOKE. I said, "I hear you were Mom's teacher once!" NO answer, of course! He didn't even flinch!!! So, I just started talking!!! I told him about things I have learned in school. After I began talking, I couldn't stop.

Mrs. Findley checked in on us every 15 minutes or so, and she had a goofy smile on her face. Finally, I had to leave, and Mrs. Findley thanked me for coming over, slipped me a cookie, and I said GOODBYE to Mr. Baxter. HE SAID NOTHING, of course! It was an experience. HOWEVER, I DON'T KNOW if I learned ANYTHING about myself like you said I would.

g2g ttyl,
Jordon

Subject: Opening your eyes
From: Bartholomew Pennington <barthpenn@heaven.org>
Date: Tues, 17 June 2003 18:20:11
To: jordonmink@intelweb.com

Dear Jordon,

That was very kind of you to pay a visit to Mr. Baxter.

What you learned about yourself today, Jordon, is that compassion is a choice. You chose to have compassion.

Too often mortals on Earth avoid situations that make them feel uncomfortable. They do not wish to get involved. Often they are selfish. Let your conscience guide your way and compassion will open your eyes.

Sincerely,
Bartholomew Pennington
Angel, 2nd Order
Cloud Nine, Heaven

From: Jordon Mink <jordonmink@intelweb.com>
To: barthpenn@heaven.org
Sent: Thurs, 19 June 2003 20:23:57
Subject: Grandma

Hey BART,

I went over to my Grandma's apartment yesterday and stayed overnight!!! It was just the two of us. It was FUN!

Grandma took me to a park part of the day, and then she drove us around and pointed out places from her childhood. FUNNY, I never think about Grandma once being a kid. DUH!!! I paid attention to everything she said.

Know what was kinda weird??? Most of the places she pointed to were NO LONGER THERE!!! She pointed to an empty field where her school USED to be. A new house now sits where the house she grew up in ONCE was. She even pointed to places in the city where there used to be barns, and woods, and a pond. I never knew THAT! And, it's ALL GONE!! NOW there are malls, fast food places and gas stations!

It made me feel kinda scared, BART. It was like everything Grandma ever knew was GONE except her memories!!

Is THAT pretty much where we END UP, BART . . . just a bunch of memories with NOTHING to point at anymore? If so, I NEVER WANNA GROW OLD!!!!!

I gotta start packing tomorrow for my stay at the Broken Arrow Penitentiary. UGH!!!!

g2g ttyl,
Jordon

Subject: Memories
From: Bartholomew Pennington <barthpenn@heaven.org>
Date: Thurs, 19 June 2003 20:54:19
To: jordonmink@intelweb.com

Dear Jordon,

Special memories are gifts we pass on to others. Your Grandmother wasn't pointing at things that are gone. She was directing your attention to things that are still there in her mind. It is her gift to you, so cherish it.

I've been gone from Earth for years, and there is a small plot on a grassy hill under a tree which has a tombstone with my name on it. Every once in a while people still visit me there, but I'm not there. I'm *here*. For those people who pay their respect, memories comfort them. Your Grandmother's memories comfort her, too, so don't feel sad.

Our memory is the book of our journey in life. Some of the pages we write; other pages are written for us. Not all memories will be happy ones. But the richest memories you will ever have are those you plant. An act of compassion today will become tomorrow's comforting memory.

Plant your memories today, and they will guide you to where you are going in life. The real secret to life's journey is not where you've been but where you're headed.

And if my memory is correct, *you* are headed to camp! LOL! Have fun at the Penitentiary!

Sincerely,
Bartholomew Pennington
Angel, 2nd Order
Cloud Nine, Heaven

P.S. – Remember to write if you have access to a computer!

---

kevin scott collier

From: Jordon Mink <jordonmink@intelweb.com>
To: barthpenn@heaven.org
Sent: Fri, 20 June 2003 20:13:27
Subject: I'm very CRABBY!!!

Hey BART,

I'm all PACKED and NOT in a very good mood! I'd ADVISE
YOU not even to write me back tonight. I do not need any more
of your colorful advice.

I will write you at camp. YEAH, they have a computer I can use.

g2g ttyl,
Jordon

From: Guest <campbrokenarrow@vista.net>
To: barthpenn@heaven.org
Sent: Sun, 22 June 2003 20:23:14
Subject: I'm in the penitentiary

Hey BART,

It's me, JORDON!!! I'm in prison. OK??? HELLLLLLPPPP!!!
Break me outta here!!!! LOL I arrived here Saturday A.M.

HERE ARE THE STATS:
There are 4 boys to every cabin, and my cabin is named Saber
Tooth. My roommates are Matt Sturgis, Tyler Madison, and
Brandon Fischer (a loser!). Tyler is really quiet, and I don't
think he likes it here. Matt can speak a whole sentence in a
belch!!! WAY COOL! Brandon took the best bunk by the
window, and he cuts in line at meal times. He is a snob and a
TROUBLEMAKER!!!

MEALS ARE LIKE THIS:
Breakfast is OK – eggs, toast and pancakes. Lunch is the best –
mostly sandwiches and snacks. Dinner is barf – they served
canned peas tonight and it was gross. One kid named John
flung a spoonful of peas at Brandon. It was pretty funny!

There are a bunch of counselors here. Ours is named Mr. Davis.
He is really nice and tells jokes.

TOMORROW 12 of us are going with Mr. Davis on a nature
hike. We have backpacks and will sleep on a big hill Monday
night, so I won't be able to write you until Tuesday night. OK?

Someone ran a kid's underwear up the flagpole yesterday. I'm
GLAD it wasn't MY underwear!!!! LOL

g2g ttyl,
Jordon

From: Guest <campbrokenarrow@vista.net>
To: barthpenn@heaven.org
Sent: Tues, 24 June 2003 20:41:22
Subject: I feel the pain!!!!

Hey BART,

Every bone in my body hurts today!!!!! Our nature trip was more like a survival course. The mosquitoes and flies ate more than I did!!!

TROUBLEMAKER Brandon wasn't so much trouble on this trip. He whined a lot when we started out but shut up when everyone called him a SISSY!!! I found out Tyler likes to draw like I do. I'll ask him to draw something while we're here.

On the trip we looked at wildflowers and Mr. Davis explained what they were. We looked under logs for salamanders too, and I got to hold one!! They are REEEEEEALLY COOOOOL! They are like little lizards. We saw a blue racer snake too.

There was a small stream on the big hill where we set up camp, and we all washed up in it. The water was freezing and I went in FIRST!!! After that we worked building a campfire, then we sat around in the dark and told scary stories. Bryce told the BEST story. It was about a werewolf! While Bryce was telling it, Matt sneaked up behind Brandon and said "BOOO", and Brandon SCREAMED!! WHAT A NERD!!!

We came back to camp a few hours ago. Gotta sweep the cabin and then go gather wood with the other Saber Tooth dudes.

Mr. Davis says that tomorrow we're hanging out at Lake Arrowhead. There's a rope you can swing on out over the lake and a raft with a diving board. I'm supposed to help out in the Mess Hall kitchen after that. I HOPE they don't have canned peas for dinner tomorrow!!! YUCK!!!!!

g2g ttyl,
Jordon

From: Guest <campbrokenarrow@vista.net>
To: barthpenn@heaven.org
Sent: Wed, 25 June 2003 20:07:58
Subject: A Mess Hall all right!!!

Hey BART,

About 20 of us swam and played in Lake Arrowhead today. Mr. Davis and Mr. Keeter were with us. I swung on that rope over the water and let go about a billion times! I let out a Tarzan yell!!! There was a raft with a diving board on it. I did back flips off it. I even taught Brandon how to do a back flip. I kinda stayed close to Brandon because he can't swim all that well, but he doesn't want others to know.

Tyler drew a few pictures in the sand with a stick. Bryce says he wants to write a book someday about werewolves. I drew him a couple pictures of werewolves after we got back to camp. Bryce says he wants me to draw the pictures for his book.

I know why they call it a MESS HALL! It's a mess all right!!!! A big lady with red hair named Miss Sophia is the Mess Hall cook. I didn't see her cook ANYTHING!!!! All she did was yell at the kitchen help and taste the food.

I didn't cook ANYTHING either! They just gave me stuff to wash and polish. LAME!!! It was boring and stupid. Sophia gave me a nickname – BOBBLEHEAD! I'm not sure I like that, but I'm keeping my mouth shut!

Friday we have to pick a partner for a project we all have to do. We won't be told what the project is until after we pick our partner.

VERY STRANGE!!!!

g2g ttyl,
Jordon

From: Guest <campbrokenarrow@vista.net>
To: barthpenn@heaven.org
Sent: Thurs, 26 June 2003 20:31:25
Subject: Brandon is a pain

Hey BART,

Ever since I was nice to Brandon at Lake Arrowhead, he's been following me around. Tyler and Matt DO NOT LIKE THIS at all!!! So, this afternoon, Matt, Tyler and I took off to go exploring and look for more salamanders. We looked behind us, and there's Brandon tagging along.

If I have to be stuck with this nerd the whole time I'm here, I WILL GO CRAZY!!!!

Everyone was talking about THE BIG PROJECT which is supposed to be a secret. Bryce said he heard it was capturing a bear. Yeah, RIGHT! No way!!! A boy named Jacob said we'd have to carve totem poles which might be true. I don't know. A skinny tall kid named Kyle said the BIG PROJECT is trying to get Miss Sophia to SMILE!!! LOL

Whatever it is, unless Tyler or Matt picks me as their partner, I'll end up being picked last for sure. I fear Tyler or Matt will pick each other; then I will be the last one picked again. They are still kinda miffed at me for being nice to Brandon yesterday.

There's another campfire tonight, and I am telling a scary story I made up today about zombies!

g2g ttyl,
Jordon

From: Guest <campbrokenarrow@vista.net>
To: barthpenn@heaven.org
Sent: Fri, 27 June 2003 20:24:13
Subject: Guess what I did?

Hey BART,

I DID SOMETHING I'M SURE I WILL REGRET!!!

This afternoon all the boys from all of the cabins were assembled near the flagpole. When Mr. Keeter called out a name, that person got to choose a partner for the BIG PROJECT. My name was called third so there were a lot of boys to pick from. BUT GUESS WHO I SAID????

BRANDON FISCHER!!!!! DUH!!!! I could just die!!! WHAT was I thinking????

Brandon was standing in that circle with his head down. He KNEW no one was going to pick him! Everyone HATES him!!!! Then when they called my name, Brandon glanced at me, and then hung his head down again. BART, I KNOW THAT LOOK!!! I've been there, done that! Some voice inside of me said I HAD to do it.

Then Mr. Davis announced what the BIG PROJECT is. We have one week to do it. GUESS WHAT IT IS????

We have to fly a kite! Is that stupid or what? After that announcement, I wanted to talk to Brandon. He had kitchen duty tonight, so he had to hurry off.

We went for a run after dinner tonight. I still haven't talked to Brandon yet. I think Sophia's cooking made him sick!!! LOL!

We're supposed to get the details on the kite project tonight at the campfire. BIG DEAL!!!! BORRRRRRIIIIIING!!!!

g2g ttyl,
Jordon

---

kevin scott collier   73

From: Guest <campbrokenarrow@vista.net>
To: barthpenn@heaven.org
Sent: Sun, 29 June 2003 13:47:14
Subject: Go fly a kite!!!

Hey BART,

Sorry I didn't write yesterday! A large group of us went
exploring with Mr. Davis and Mr. Keeter. We shared binoculars
and watched birds. KINDA BORING. Then we climbed a big hill
and saw an eagle's nest! I found an eagle feather lying on the
ground, but I didn't keep it because it's illegal to even have a
feather from that bird!

Tyler and Matt don't like me anymore, and Bryce doesn't talk to
me now because I think he was jealous of my zombie story the
other night. WHATEVER! I know Matt and Tyler are still mad
at me for not picking one of them as my partner. AND TO
MAKE MATTERS WORSE, now Brandon is right by my side
always! Some kids are snickering, and a couple called me
names. What a bunch of LOSERS!!!

I found out that the kite project isn't such a joke after all! It's
NOT just FLYING a kite. IT'S BUILDING ONE too! And it
can't be diamond shaped either!!! We have to make our own
design, build it out of wood and paper, and paint it to look like
something. The Camp supplies the materials.

Brandon says it will be a piece of cake. I'm not SO SURE about
that. That dude needs a reality check.

I have been watching over my shoulder when I write to you
BART! OK? So, everything's cool.

Tomorrow we're going back to Lake Arrowhead! AWESOME!!!

g2g ttyl,
Jordon

Hey BART,

This afternoon Brandon and I had time alone in Saber Tooth to go over this kite project. It turns out I may have picked the best partner of all! GO FIGURE!!! Brandon's says his Dad is a carpenter, and they build stuff for fun all of the time. There is a pile of precut wood sticks in the camp barn we can use for this project and big rolls of newsprint paper to cover the frame. We have the sheet with the guidelines for the project and have been brainstorming!

THE RULES are kinda like this:
You cannot make the kite a diamond shape.
You have to design your own kite.
You have to paint your kite to resemble something.
You CAN'T test your kite out in advance to see if it flies!!!

The only time Brandon and I will see if our kite flies is on Friday afternoon when we all meet at the bottom of Weeping Hill for the competition! YOU HEARD RIGHT!!! WE have to design something we BELIEVE will fly without knowing!!!

IF OUR KITE DOES FLY, that's only PART of it! There is a huge tree with a billion branches at the top of that hill, and we have to get our kite to fly over the top of that tree. GUESS WHAT????? That tree is a kite graveyard!!! It's full of shredded paper, wooden frames and a trillion pieces of string hanging from it!! They even have a name for that monster!!! It's called THE TREACHEROUS TREE!!!

I drew some pictures of ideas of what our kite could look like. Brandon tells me what I should change in the drawings so that our kite WILL fly. I wanted to make the kite look like a pterodactyl, but Brandon said "No way!" Brandon said it would be too unsteady and the wings might break!! F.Y.I. – a pterodactyl is an extinct flying reptile. OK???

Brandon and I are going to brainstorm by the campfire again tonight. I'll let you know what we come up with!!!

g2g ttyl,
Jordon

From: Guest <campbrokenarrow@vista.net>
To: Barthpenn@heaven.org
Sent: Tues, 01 July 2003 20:22:08
Subject: Fly like and EAGLE!!!

Hey BART,

Last night at the campfire, Brandon and I were talking about the eagles nest we saw. That's when it hit us! Our kite is gonna LOOK LIKE AN EAGLE!!! (Hopefully fly like one too!)

We went swimming at Lake Arrowhead this morning, but Brandon and I wanted to get back as soon as we could!!! As soon as we got back, we went to the barn and got all of the right sized sticks Brandon says we need.

We're working from two drawings I made. ONE DRAWING is a wood skeleton of the bird. Brandon says IT WILL be sturdy!!! The OTHER DRAWING is what the eagle will look like once finished and I paint the kite.

We're gonna start building it tomorrow morning. Brandon and I are so excited we won't get to sleep tonight! I'm sure we will be getting the "evil eye" from roommates Tyler and Matt. They both have been VERY quiet! They aren't speaking to one another EITHER!!! Both have different partners and EVERYONE is VERY secretive about what they will do.

Tyler and I give each other stares BIG TIME. We're both artists. Whatever that dude is gonna paint on his kite isn't gonna beat my eagle!!! EVEN IF IT DOES, I bet NO ONE else here has a partner who can BUILD things from wood!!! SO EVEN IF Tyler has a better-looking kite, it STILL HAS TO FLY, or he and his partner are OUT!!!

OF COURSE if our eagle DOES fly, WE have to get it OVER THAT TREE, and it seems to look LARGER every day.

g2g ttyl,
Jordon

---

kevin scott collier

From: Guest <campbrokenarrow@vista.net>
To: barthpenn@heaven.org
Sent: Wed, 02 July 2003 20:52:13
Subject: Things are getting weird!

Hey BART,

It's been a LOOOOOOOOOOOONG day!!! LOL
We did lots of cool stuff . . . swimming, hiking, blah blah blah!

LET'S CUT TO THE CHASE AND GET RIGHT TO THE
KITE!!!!!

Matt and his partner, as well as TWO OTHER TEAMS, were
caught TEST FLYING their kites this afternoon! THEY ARE
OUT!!!
THAT IS...
O
U
T
OUTTA HERE!!! Hahahahahahahahahahahahahahaha!

Matt is FUMING!!! Tyler and I kinda lightened up a little and
were talking. WE were laughing about Matt getting the BOOT!
THEN things changed!!!

Brandon and I showed Tyler and his partner, Douglas, our kite
frame and the drawing I did of what it will look like when it's
finished. Tyler and Douglas then showed us THEIR frame and
the drawings of what their kite will look like when it's finished.
Tyler's kite is A BAT!!! NO KIDDING!!! (It looks VERY cool on
paper BUT will it FLY?)

NOW Brandon and I AREN'T TALKING to Tyler or Douglas
ANYMORE!!! I THINK eagles eat bats for lunch!!!

Almost all of the other kids have their kites done ALREADY!!!
It's like they were just slapped together!! Brandon says those
kites are JUNK!!! They're nothing worth talking about!!! BUT
Tyler's kite has me CONCERNED! Brandon says it may FLY!!!

UGH!!! Brandon's NOT sure!

I gotta get out to the campfire. I can't leave Brandon alone to fend off the BAT SQUAD!

g2g ttyl.
Jordon

From: Guest <campbrokenarrow@vista.net>
To: barthpenn@heaven.org
Sent: Thurs, 03 July 2003 20:34:45
Subject: Eagle

Hey BART,

Today was a LOT of work but we DID IT!!! Our kite is DONE!
We haven't seen Tyler's kite and he hasn't seen ours! They have
their kite stashed in the REC HALL somewhere, and we have
ours hidden in a loft in the barn.

I still have some more painting to do tonight! I wanna get the
wings JUST RIGHT!! Mr. Davis hooked up a floodlight in the
loft but says we have to be to bed by 11:00. NO CAMPFIRE
TONIGHT for Brandon and me; we have work to do!!!

During the afternoon, I was talking to a counselor named Mr.
Beecham about the BIG Kite Flying Event tomorrow. He said
the idea for flying kites here at Camp Broken Arrow goes back
40 years. THEN he said something that kinda shocked me!!!

Mr. Beecham said the last kite to make it over the TOP of the
TREACHEROUS TREE was ten years ago!!! That's the YEAR I
WAS BORN!!! That's a LONG time!!!

I mean come on! HOW stupid is that??? Why even have a kite
building contest with a goal like that? I asked Mr. Beecham
that, and he said it's not really about kites. It's about challenge
and teamwork!!!

YEAH, RIGHT!!! Sounds more like it's about failure to me!! I
asked him why they would even keep a silly project like this
when the tree eats all of the kites. Mr. Beecham just smiled and
said "BECAUSE IT IS POSSIBLE."

Brandon and I aren't gonna let that TREE get us!!!

I'm putting the last coat of paint on the eagle tonight and it
WILL fly tomorrow!! Tyler's BAT WING is gonna be TREE

FOOD!!!

Wish us luck, BART!!!

g2g ttyl,
Jordon

From: Guest <campbrokenarrow@vista.net>
To: barthpenn@heaven.org
Sent: Fri, 04 July 2003 20:02:51
Subject: It's OVER

Hey BART,

GUESS WHAT I FORGOT???? I was so busy with the kite I forgot today is the 4^(TH) OF JULY!!! There's a farewell campfire tonight, and there is supposed to be some fireworks!!! BANG, ZOOM!!!!

ABOUT the BIG Kite Flying Event, I'll give you the play by play. OK?

We all brought our kites to the bottom of Weeping Hill. The wind was good, and Brandon and I were pumped up! Mr. Davis and Mr. Beecham picked out who would go first. It was clear they saved the BEST for LAST, so Brandon and I got EXCITED!

GUESS WHAT??? Two teams got booted right away because they built diamond shaped kites! DUH! Didn't they read the rules???? MOST of the kites before us NEVER GOT OFF THE GROUND!!! Some of them fell apart on takeoff, but that was OK because even the kids who made them started to laugh!!

WELL . . . it came down to just Tyler and Douglas and Brandon and me. I could see Brandon sweating, and he was really quiet. I began to wonder if he was SO SURE of what we built anymore.

So, Tyler's BAT WING takes off and shoots straight up into the sky!! Brandon and I are both sweating now! Then, as it reaches the top of the TREACHEROUS TREE, it started to spin out! IT WAS LIKE A STUNT KITE or something!!! It came down so fast it almost hit Mr. Beecham in the head!! OUTTA HERE!!! It smashed into a billion pieces! (That BAT needed some RADAR! LOL)

OUR EAGLE KITE went last... Brandon let me fly it!!! HE wanted me to! It took off like an eagle, and as it gained height, I backed away from the bottom of Weeping Hill to better see the top of the TREACHEROUS TREE.

Just as it started to reach the top of the tree, a wing got snagged in a branch!!! Brandon swallowed HARD, and said, "GIVE IT A TUG!" I did, BUT the kite was still stuck!!! So I freaked out and yanked the string. BIG MISTAKE!!! THE LINE BROKE!!! It was all over THAT FAST!!

But, it DOESN'T MATTER; Brandon and I know that kite WAS headed over that tree! We didn't have to see it go over to know it. KNOW what I mean??? At least our kite didn't crash to the ground like Tyler's BAT WING!!!

So that's DONE, and CAMP IS TOO after tonight. Dad is picking me up tomorrow morning.

OH, I did write my parents too while I was here but NOT as MUCH as you, BART!

It will be nice hearing from you again when I get back home.

Our farewell campfire and fireworks start soon! I actually miss your spewing!!

g2g ttyl,
Jordon

P.S. - I did have fun here . . . whether I LIKED IT OR NOT!

From: Jordon Mink <jordonmink@intelweb.com>
To: barthpenn@heaven.org
Sent: Sat, 05 July 2003 15:37:19
Subject: I'm back home now

Hey BART,

I'm all unpacked and it's good to be HOME! I even missed my brat sister and gave her a hug!!! YUCK! Mom is making me my favorite dinner tonight, PIZZA!!! Dad fibbed and said we were having canned peas!!!

My room sure looks good after sleeping on a bunk in a cabin for two weeks!!

I gave Brandon my email address at camp. I hope he writes me. I don't have his! My Dad said I could have him over to visit, and he even told Brandon that when he met him this morning. Brandon is supposed to ask his parents to see if it is OK. Brandon lives in Kenton which is about 20 miles from here.

OH, YOU JUST GOTTA HEAR THIS... Early this morning while I was still at camp, I was awakened in Saber Tooth cabin by a bunch of kids rushing in yelling about that tree on Weeping Hill. They scared my roommates and me to death!!! They said "YOU GOTTA SEE THIS!!!" So we all rushed outside in our pajamas. YOU'RE NOT GONNA BELIEVE THIS but there it was. OUR EAGLE KITE was flying in place high over that tree!!!

Somehow during the night the wind must have shook it loose, and it took flight again! The end of the string had wrapped around a branch which held it in place!!! It was AN AWESOME sight!!! EVERYONE just stood there and stared! Mr. Beecham said he'd never seen anything like it!!!

"IT IS POSSIBLE," just like he said!

It's kinda strange that Dad and I didn't get to meet Brandon's Dad. Brandon just ran over to their car when it pulled up and

---

yelled goodbye!!! WEIRD!!!

I HOPE I GET a letter from YOU TONIGHT!!! Yeah, I missed
you, BART.

g2g ttyl,
Jordon

Subject: Paper Eagles
From: Bartholomew Pennington <barthpenn@heaven.org>
Date: Sat, 05 July 2003 16:01:20
To: jordonmink@intelweb.com

Dear BOBBLEHEAD,

(Just a joke. All right?)

I read every letter you sent me and enjoyed sharing in your adventures.

I do have a question. Before your kite actually flew above the tree, did you not first *believe* it would? Remember, Jordon, belief is a powerful thing. All things are possible once you believe.

Concerning Brandon: have patience. Brandon will write. You two are kindred spirits now.

Take care,
Bartholomew Pennington
Angel, 2nd Order
Cloud Nine, Heaven

barthpenn@heaven.org

From: Jordon Mink <jordonmink@intelweb.com>
To: barthpenn@heaven.org
Sent: Sat, 05 July 2003 20:14:51
Subject: Thinking about Brandon

Hey BART,

BOBBLEHEAD. Yeah, right! I should fling a spoonful of rotten peas at Cloud Nine for that!!

I have been thinking about how Brandon and I became friends. I wonder if the reason I went to camp was so I could meet Brandon. I didn't want to go to camp at all, but if I hadn't, I never would have met him. There were about 30 kids at the camp, 8 cabins in all. What were the chances I'd end up in the same cabin with Brandon? And, then there's the KITE!!! What are the chances that I would pick the one boy in the entire camp that really knew how to build a kite that would fly???

I mean when a series of events all takes place that, what would you call it???

g2g ttyl,
Jordon

Subject: ?
From: Bartholomew Pennington <barthpenn@heaven.org>
Date: Sat, 05 July 2003 20:25:47
To: jordonmink@intelweb.com

Jordon,

MEANT TO BE!

Sincerely,
Bartholomew Pennington
Angel, 2nd Order
Cloud Nine, Heaven

From: Jordon Mink <jordonmink@intelweb.com>
To: barthpenn@heaven.org
Sent: Sun, 06 July, 2003 16:24:13
Subject: BAD news

Hey BART,

Mr. Baxter died while I was away at camp. Mom and Dad didn't tell me until after church today. I wanted to visit him right after church.

Now he is gone forever.

Tomorrow I hafta go over there to cut his grass! What will I say to Mrs. Findley???

I DON'T KNOW WHAT I AM GOING TO SAY.

Maybe if I hadn't gone to camp, I could have said goodbye.

g2g ttyl,
Jordon

Subject: Mr. Baxter
From: Bartholomew Pennington <barthpenn@heaven.org>
Date: Mon, 07 July 2003 07:05:37
To: jordonmink@intelweb.com

Dear Jordon,

May I share a secret with you?

The great ocean liner Titanic had four smoke stacks, but only three actually spewed smoke. The fourth one, at the stern of the ship, was ornamental.

Take care,
Bartholomew Pennington
Angel, 2nd Order
Cloud Nine, Heaven

From: Jordon Mink <jordonmink@intelweb.com>
To: barthpenn@heaven.org
Sent: Mon, 07 July, 2003 08:24:59
Subject: Hello????

Hey BART,

WHERE DID YOU HEAR THAT FROM???

g2g,
Jordon

Subject: Re: Hello????
From: Bartholomew Pennington <barthpenn@heaven.org>
Date: Mon, 07 July 2003 08:27:45
To: jordonmink@intelweb.com

Jordon,

Let's see if I can catch you still online.

Isn't this something that *you told* Mr. Baxter the last time you paid him a visit?

Bartholomew Pennington
Angel, 2nd Order
Cloud Nine, Heaven

From: Jordon Mink <jordonmink@intelweb.com>
To: barthpenn@heaven.org
Sent: Mon, 07 July, 2003 08:34:19
Subject: HOW???

WELL, YEAH, but HOW do YOU KNOW this?????

Jordon

Subject: Re: HOW???
From: Bartholomew Pennington <barthpenn@heaven.org>
Date: Mon, 07 July 2003 08:45:38
To: jordonmink@intelweb.com

Jordon,

Mr. Baxter told me.

I paid him a visit when he arrived here. We had a very nice conversation.

Don't ever think your presence in the company of another does not matter. Even when you may think you cannot be making a difference, you may be making all the difference in the world.

Now, don't you have a lawn to cut?

Take care,
Bartholomew Pennington
Angel, 2nd Order
Cloud Nine, Heaven

From: Karen Fischer <kfischer@intelweb.com>
To: jordonmink@intelweb.com
Sent: Mon, 07 July 2003 17:45:18
Subject: It's me, Brandon!

Dear Jordon,

Wasn't that something about our kite on Saturday? We ruled, dude! Know what's funny? I told my buddies and they thought I was making it up. Whatever!

Have you asked your parents yet when I can come and stay at your place? Mom and Dad don't have a problem with it. I can come ANYTIME!

Let me know!

Bye,
Brandon Fischer

P.S. If you still have any of those drawings you did of our eagle kite, can you send me one in the mail? I could hang it on my bedroom wall and never forget that day.

My address is: 2967 Maplegrove, Kenton, WI 55555

From: Jordon Mink <jordonmink@intelweb.com>
To: kfischer@intelweb.com
Sent: Mon, 07 July, 2003 19:20:13
Subject: FOR BRANDON

Hey BRANDON,

My Mom and Dad said you could come over this weekend!!!!
Dad's calling your house tonight to set up the whole deal.
COOL!

My Mom said she would mail off a drawing of the kite at the
post office tomorrow. You'll get it the next day. OK, DUDE?

When you stay here, you can sleep in MY BED, and I will use
my sleeping bag on the floor. You can even CUT IN LINE at
mealtime. OK??? LOL

This is gonna be AWESOME!!!

g2g ttyl,
Jordon

From: Jordon Mink <jordonmink@intelweb.com>
To: barthpenn@heaven.org
Sent: Tues, 08 July 2003 08:24:59
Subject: Brandon's coming over

Hey BART,

My Dad talked to Brandon's Mom last night, and he can come over this Friday. Brandon's Uncle Ken is working construction a couple miles from here, so he'll be dropping Brandon off here around 4:00. Mom and Dad said Brandon can stay until Monday afternoon. After that, Dad and I are going on a FATHER AND SON fishing trip alone.

I don't know how I'll be able to email you while Brandon is here, but I'll figure SOMETHING out to let you know what we're both up to!!! LOL

I'm going over to Mrs. Findley's this afternoon. I'm gonna help her with her garden. It will feel weird to be there now, but Mrs. Findley's cool!!! Did I tell you she wears a huge, silly straw hat when she picks vegetables in her little garden? She always gives me vegetables to bring home to Mom. YUCK! (I HATE VEGETABLES!!!)

I wish I could tell her that her Dad is in Heaven. But I won't. Somehow I think she already knows.

g2g ttyl,
Jordon

From: Jordon Mink <jordonmink@intelweb.com>
To: barthpenn@heaven.org
Sent: Tues, 08 July 2003 18:37:23
Subject: Mrs. Findley

Hey BART,

After I helped Mrs. Findley pick green beans, she wanted me to help her move some stuff in her basement. I said, NO PROBLEM-O!!!!

It was like 100 degrees outdoors today, and the basement was nice and cool! You wouldn't believe all of the BOOKS Mr. Baxter had!!! He liked to read a lot. While I was digging though a box, I found a book WRITTEN BY MR. BAXTER!!!

Mrs. Findley said it was published in 1962, and she wanted me to HAVE IT! She said she had more copies of it. When I opened the cover, I noticed it was autographed. It read; "Rejoice on your journey, Henry T. Baxter." WOW!

Mrs. Findley explained these were leftover copies from book signings Mr. Baxter did. He often signed many copies in advance. KNOW what is SPOOKY? The ink was still damp on the inscription and autograph. FREAKY!!!

I asked Mrs. Findley how many OTHER books her Dad had written, and she said that he'd only written this one. She said, "Dad claimed he said everything he had to say in that book." The book is titled "FINGERPRINTS", and I'm gonna start reading it tonight!

SO DON'T WRITE ME TONIGHT!!!
I'LL BE BUSY READING!!!!   LOL

g2g ttyl,
Jordon

From: Karen Fischer <kfischer@intelweb.com>
To: jordonmink@intelweb.com
Sent: Wed, 09 July 2003 12:25:56
Subject: It's me, Brandon!

Dear Jordon,

I got your drawing today! VERY Cool! I bet it's gonna be worth big $$$ some day! I already hung it on my bedroom wall!

Thanks, DUDE!

I heard your Dad talked to my Mom on the phone, and I guess everything's set for Friday.

See you then.

Bye,
Brandon

From: Jordon Mink <jordonmink@intelweb.com>
To: kfischer@intelweb.com
Sent: Wed, 09 July 2003 15:42:13
Subject: FOR BRANDON

Hey BRANDON,

I have LOTS OF PLANS for us!!!!

My parents are cool and you will like them. Mom will probably be overly nice because I don't have guests often. Dad is easy going. You can meet my friend, Peter, who lives down the street. I want you to meet Mrs. Findley too; we can probably shake her down for some fresh baked cookies!

W A R N I N G . . .
LOSER ALERT! LOSER ALERT!
I have a sister named Erin. She is 8. She is extremely irritating. She likes to butt in all of the time whenever Peter comes over. She will try to NOSE AROUND while you are here, so just IGNORE her!!!

Can you bring your bike? ASK your Mom or Dad, OK???

See you FRIDAY!!!

g2g ttyl,
Jordon

From: Jordon Mink <jordonmink@intelweb.com>
To: barthpenn@heaven.org
Sent: Thurs, 10 July 2003 22:01:28
Subject: FINGERPRINTS

Hey BART,

Brandon comes over to stay tomorrow afternoon, and I'm HYPER about it!!!!

BART, isn't life STRANGE??? BRANDON was THE LAST PERSON at camp I should have made friends with!!! Wanna know something else that is STRANGE??? I have read about 80 pages of Mr. Baxter's "FINGERPRINTS" book so far, and it's not a CRIME NOVEL AT ALL!! I thought it was about detectives looking for bad guys and stuff.

"FINGERPRINTS" is about ACTS OF KINDNESS. On page 67, Mr. Baxter wrote, "We leave traces of ourselves on others, and they leave traces of themselves on us. By the end of our lives, we have become a collection of everyone who ever loved us."

I have a funny feeling Mr. Baxter wanted me to find this book in his basement. I think this copy was meant for ME.

I'll log on and write you when I can over the weekend. It will be kinda hard with my guest here!!!

You know BART, you really should work on getting some friends! LOL

g2g ttyl,
Jordon

Subject: Re: FINGERPRINTS
From: Bartholomew Pennington <barthpenn@heaven.org >
Date: Thurs, 10 July 2003 22:16:16
To: jordonmink@intelweb.com

Dear Jordon,

Have a great time with Brandon!

I met Mr. Baxter once in 1962 at a book signing for
Fingerprints. His book inspired me as a mortal. So, perhaps
while you were forming a friendship with Brandon down there, I
was forming one with Mr. Baxter up here. Perhaps I *have* been
working on "getting some new friends."

And perhaps it is late, and *you* should be in *bed*!

Sincerely,
Bartholomew Pennington
Angel, 2nd Order
Cloud Nine, Heaven

From: Jordon Mink <jordonmink@intelweb.com>
To: barthpenn@heaven.org
Sent: Thurs, 10 July 2003 22:30:22
Subject: Whatever!

Good night, loser! LOL.

Jordon

From: Jordon Mink <jordonmink@intelweb.com>
To: barthpenn@heaven.org
Sent: Sat, 12 July 2003 18:20:45
Subject: Brandon's here

Hey BART,

Brandon left with Dad to pick up a pizza, so I only have a few minutes to write. Brandon's kinda shy around my parents, but he REALLY likes it here. I was worried he'd think my bedroom was too small, but he said it was really cool. My sister thinks Brandon's CUTE! She's showing off in front of him. UGH!!!!!

This morning we helped Mrs. Findley with her garage sale. I'm glad Brandon got to meet her. I'd told Mrs. Findley about Brandon this week. They hit it off real well!!! Brandon and I also went over to my friend Peter's house and played a little basketball in his driveway. Peter thought Brandon was cool too.

Brandon and I built a tiny wooden sailboat this afternoon. Dad is taking us to Crystal Channel tomorrow afternoon to go swimming. We'll get to play with our sailboat too. My irritating sister wanted to come along, but Dad said, "NO!" Mom is taking Erin over to Grandma's. Hahahahaha!!!!!

Brandon doesn't talk much about his family and doesn't WANT TO either! I wonder why? Do you know what's kinda weird? The man who dropped Brandon off yesterday afternoon was the SAME man who picked him up from Camp Broken Arrow! So that wasn't Brandon's Dad who I saw pick him up from camp! It was his Uncle Ken. I wonder why Brandon said the man who's really his Uncle was his Dad. Maybe I just heard wrong.

I should sign off before they get back just to be safe.

g2g ttyl,
Jordon

From: Jordon Mink <jordonmink@intelweb.com>
To: barthpenn@heaven.org
Sent: Sun, 13 July 2003 08:15:42
Subject: Problem

Hey BART,

I have a few minutes before we head off to Church.

Brandon's outdoors tossing a ball with Dad.

Something weird is going on, BART. I don't know what
Brandon's problem is. I thought this weekend would be a great
way to get to know him better. But the closer I get, the more
distant he becomes.

Maybe he doesn't like me. Maybe this WASN'T meant to be.

g2g ttyl,
Jordon

Subject: Re: Problem
From: Bartholomew Pennington <barthpenn@heaven.org>
Date: Sun, 13 July 2003 08:20:16
To: jordonmink@intelweb.com

Dear Jordon,

Have patience. This *was* meant to be.

Sincerely,
Bartholomew Pennington
Angel, 2nd Order
Cloud Nine, Heaven

From: Jordon Mink <jordonmink@intelweb.com>
To: barthpenn@heaven.org
Sent: Mon, 14 July 2003 17:42:12
Subject: The friendship is OVER!!!

Hey BART,

It was a NIGHTMARE!!!

Brandon's Uncle Ken just picked him up, and I'm GLAD he's outta here!! I am never speaking to that creep again!!! I should have known better. My first impression of him the first day at camp was RIGHT! He is a snob and NO friend of mine!

Things were fun at Crystal Channel yesterday until I asked, "WHEN can I come to YOUR HOUSE?"Brandon got all mad and said, "You are NEVER coming to MY HOUSE, you are NOT WELCOME!" Things got pretty QUIET after that, let ME tell YOU!! My Dad knew something was up.

Most of today before Brandon left he rode his bike around my neighborhood and talked with my giggling showoff sister!!! That made me REALLY MAD!!!

I know what's going on, BART! I'm NOT GOOD ENOUGH to meet Brandon's snob friends! Well, I will save him the embarrassment. I'd never go to his house EVEN if he changed his mind! I wouldn't want to cause MR. PERFECT any trouble. My EX-FRIEND is back where he belongs, in SNOBville!

Do you have any pearls of wisdom for this one, BART??? Come on, I'm sure you can think of something SMART to say. You know . . . some GRAND reason why this friendship came apart. Hey, maybe I'll find the answer in Mr. Baxter's book! LOL! Yeah, right!!!

Do you know what's worse than being angry? BEING HURT!!!

g2g ttyl,
Jordon

---

kevin scott collier

Subject: About Brandon
From: Bartholomew Pennington <barthpenn@heaven.org>
Date: Mon, 14 July 2003 18:12:47
To: jordonmink@intelweb.com

Dear Jordon,

Don't let your emotions foster assumptions concerning Brandon.

I shouldn't tell you this, but if you approach your Father in the right way, he will likely confirm what I am about to tell you. Your father probably discovered this when he made arrangements with Brandon's mother for his visit.

You've already observed that it was Brandon's Uncle Kenneth who actually picked him up from Camp Broken Arrow. What you don't know is that it was Uncle Ken who taught Brandon woodworking skills that enabled him to construct that kite. Again, it wasn't Brandon's father.

Brandon's Father is up *here*, Jordon. He's been in Heaven since Brandon was a baby.

Your so-called "ex- friend" lives alone with his mother.

I will not tell you the reason why Brandon is reluctant to invite you over to his house. I will let you discover that for yourself.

Sincerely,
Bartholomew Pennington
Angel, 2nd Order
Cloud Nine, Heaven

From: Jordon Mink <jordonmink@intelweb.com>
To: barthpenn@heaven.org
Sent: Tues, 15 July 2003 19:21:07
Subject: I messed up

Dear BART,

I feel SO ashamed of myself.

Dad and I spent most of the day fishing at Higgins Creek. In the car on the way there, I asked Dad if he had talked to Brandon's father. Brandon's Mom, Mrs. Fischer, told Dad all about it. YOU were right, BART! She said Brandon only told me he had a Dad so I wouldn't feel sorry for him. He wanted me to think everything was OK in his life, but it's NOT!

After we left Higgins Creek, Dad said the town of Kenton was only 5 miles away. He asked, "Would you like to see where Brandon lives? We can just drive by." We found Maplegrove Road, and even Dad's eyes got big! It was a REALLY poor neighborhood. And, Brandon's address wasn't a house at all but an old rundown apartment building. Then, we saw Brandon across the street in an empty dirt lot kicking around a soccer ball. He was alone. (Brandon didn't see us.)

That's when I explained to Dad what happened at Crystal Channel Sunday afternoon. I told about how Brandon got upset and shouted at me that I would NEVER be welcome in HIS home. I told Dad how we had some pretty nasty words between us which I am ashamed of.

Dad asked if I wanted him to turn the car around, and stop. He said I could join Brandon in the lot and kick the soccer ball around with him a while. I said "No thanks." Even if I wanted to see Brandon, I'm sure he wouldn't want to see me.

I was wrong about Brandon not inviting me over to his place. It wasn't because Brandon was ashamed of ME; he thought I would be ashamed of HIM.

---

kevin scott collier

I feel terrible, BART. What should I do?

g2g ttyl,
Jordon

Subject: Advice?
From: Bartholomew Pennington <barthpenn@heaven.org>
Date: Tues, 15 July 2003 19:52:19
To: jordonmink@intelweb.com

Dear Jordon,

Material things have nothing to do with true friendships. It's not what you have, Jordon, it's who you are.

I suggest you read the *rest* of Mr. Baxter's book. He left it for you for a reason. Don't write me until you've finished it.

Sincerely,
Bartholomew Pennington
Angel, 2nd Order
Cloud Nine, Heaven

From: Jordon Mink <jordonmink@intelweb.com>
To: barthpenn@heaven.org
Sent: Sat, 19 July 2003 12:05:40
Subject: I finished the book

Hey BART,

I went over to Mrs. Findley's to cut her lawn this morning. My Mom picked some daisies from our garden for me to give her. I stopped by the corner store on the way and bought Mrs. Findley a little box of candy. When I knocked on her door, I gave her flowers and candy. She cried! I felt terrible!!! Then, she said it was a GOOD kind of cry.

She invited me inside, and the house smelled like chocolate! She was baking TONS of BROWNIES for a Church raffle. She doesn't go to our church, but I might go there JUST to BID on those brownies!!! She did give me two. YUM YUM!!!!

I finished reading "FINGERPRINTS" last night. It made me think a lot about how I have acted lately. Mr. Baxter wrote, "We leave traces of ourselves on others, and they leave traces of themselves on us." The only TRACE I left on Brandon was a mean STREAK. The book is about kindness and how we all touch one another. I don't deserve this book as I am not sure yet what true friendship is.

I just need some time alone to think.

g2g ttyl,
Jordon

Subject: Understood
From: Bartholomew Pennington <barthpenn@heaven.org>
Date: Sat, 19 July 2003 13:25:33
To: jordonmink@intelweb.com

Dear Jordon,

I'll leave you alone for a few days and then get back to you.

Take care,
Bartholomew Pennington
Angel, 2nd Order
Cloud Nine, Heaven

From: Jordon Mink <jordonmink@intelweb.com>
To: barthpenn@heaven.org
Sent: Sat, 19 July 2003 13:34:07
Subject: Thanks

Thanks for understanding, BART.

You have been here for me when it seemed like no one else was.
I appreciate that. Someone is going to be incredibly lucky when
you are appointed their Guardian Angel.

I just need to do a little soul searching. I'll be fine. I promise.

g2g,ttyl,
Jordon

\<Chapter Four\>

\<SYSTEM FAILURE\>

Subject: Feeling Better
From: Bartholomew Pennington <barthpenn@heaven.org>
Date: Wed, 23 July 2003 16:12:54
To: jordonmink@intelweb.com

Dear Jordon,

Hope you are feeling better.

Did you go to the church raffle and bid on Mrs. Findley's brownies?

LOL.

Sincerely,
Bartholomew Pennington
Angel, 2nd Order
Cloud Nine, Heaven

Subject: Want to talk?
From: Bartholomew Pennington <barthpenn@heaven.org>
Date: Thurs, 24 July 2003 16:42:13
To: jordonmink@intelweb.com

Dear Jordon,

Is the issue with Brandon still bothering you?

Would you like to talk about it?

Sincerely,
Bartholomew Pennington
Angel, 2nd Order
Cloud Nine, Heaven

Subject: (no subject)
From: Bartholomew Pennington <barthpenn@heaven.org>
Date: Fri, 25 July 2003 16:07:22
To: jordonmink@intelweb.com

Jordon,

Are you all right?

Bartholomew Pennington
Angel, 2nd Order
Cloud Nine, Heaven

Subject: URGENT
From: Bartholomew Pennington <barthpenn@heaven.org>
Date: Fri, 25 July 2003 17:22:03
To: danhillsdale@heaven.org

Hillsdale,

Get over to the Mink residence ASAP and report what you observe.

Bartholomew Pennington
Angel, 2nd Order
Cloud Nine, Heaven

Subject: At the Mink residence
From: Daniel Hillsdale <danhillsdale@heaven.org>
Date: Fri., 25 July 2003 17:45:19
To: barthpenn@heaven.org

Dear Bartholomew,

Jordon took ill Tuesday night and was rushed to the hospital. His mother, sister and Aunt are here at their home.

The conversation concerning the boy's condition is not good. Jordon IS dying.

I am presently in the boy's room on his computer doing clean up. I have already deleted the three messages you sent Jordon over the last few days. There were no others.

I checked the diary he keeps hidden under his mattress and there were no entries concerning you. However, I did find a feather used to bookmark a blank page in the diary. (It looked very suspicious!) I took it upon myself to check Jordon's feather marks on his nightstand in search of clues.

The pages with feather bookmarks correspond with verses on ANGELS! Apparently this boy was a big fan of Angels before you ever stumbled into his life! The feather in the diary corresponds with a blank page dated Friday, May 30, 2003. Just a hunch here, but could this be the day you revealed to Jordon that you were in fact an Angel?

I am headed to the hospital next. I will report back shortly.

Sincerely,
Daniel Hillsdale
3rd Order Angel, Apprentice
Earth Operative, Wisconsin USA

Subject: At the hospital
From: Daniel Hillsdale <danhillsdale@heaven.org>
Date: Fri, 25 July 2003 18:08:19
To: barthpenn@heaven.org

Dear Bartholomew,

Jordon's father and uncle are here at the hospital by his bedside. Jordon underwent some radical treatments today and doctors are waiting for the results.

F.Y.I. Jordon is in Beloit Memorial Hospital, room 57.

I must return to my other duties now.

Again the boy's computer has been scanned, and when he departs this world, there will be no trace that he ever knew you. But just to be safe, should I return to Jordon's bedroom and remove the feather from the blank page in his diary?

Sincerely,
Daniel Hillsdale
3rd Order Angel, Apprentice
Earth Operative, Wisconsin USA

Subject: Thank you
From: Bartholomew Pennington <barthpenn@heaven.org>
Date: Fri, 25 July 2003 18:12:07
To: danhillsdale@heaven.org

Dear Daniel,

Do not remove the feather from the diary. It is a secret only known to the boy.

Thank you for your assistance, and let me know if there is any change in Jordon's condition.

Sincerely,
Bartholomew Pennington
Angel, 2nd Order
Cloud Nine, Heaven

Subject: Request a miracle
From: Bartholomew Pennington <barthpenn@heaven.org>
Date: Fri, 25 July 2003 21:34:52
To: st.andrew@kingdom.org

Dearest St. Andrew,

Jordon Mink is dying, but it is not his time. If there are any miracles left to come out of Heaven today, please consider one for Jordon Mink.

Do you remember my final scroll which earned me this position on Cloud Nine? It was about pebbles, ponds, and ripples. You said it was one of the best scrolls you had read in a long time.

Perhaps I can refresh your memory with a small piece from that scroll. "Some people are pebbles striking a calm pond. Unseen and unheard, the splash goes unnoticed. But the smallest ripple can produce the greatest waves. Ripples touch us, move through us, then move beyond us. These ripples in life change us. Often these ripples are difficult to trace back to one single person. The ripple may be one unnoticed splash . . . one person who reaches far beyond himself and isn't even aware of it."

Jordon Mink is a pebble. He has struck the pond of life. The ripples are already moving, St. Andrew.

Please consider taking the issue of Jordon's fate to the highest level. Not for me but for Jordon and all of mankind.

Sincerely,
Bartholomew Pennington
Angel, 2nd Class
Cloud Nine, Heaven

Subject: Get down here
From: Daniel Hillsdale <danhillsdale@heaven.org>
Date: Sat, 26 July 2003 10:12:41
To: barthpenn@heaven.org

Dear Bartholomew,

You had better get down here. I just stopped by the hospital to check out how the treatments went for Jordon. Something happened overnight, and the boy took a sharp turn for the worse. He's going fast.

I am coming up to Cloud Nine now to cover for you.

Sincerely,
Daniel Hillsdale
3rd Order Angel, Apprentice
Earth Operative, Wisconsin USA

Subject: What IS going on?
From: Gennif Willow <genwillow@kingdom.org>
Date: Sat, 26 July 2003 13:02:38
To: barthpenn@heaven.org

Dear Bartholomew,

I just stopped by Cloud Nine to see how you were doing, and there's Hillsdale again! He wouldn't say a word. What in Heaven's name is going on? Even St. Andrew is missing!

Bartholomew, if you think all of this sneaking around is being clever, best you know your little secret about emailing the boy is out. It's all over Heaven.

You're going to be stripped of your wings for this.

Sincerely,
Gennif Willow
Angel, 2nd Order, Administrative
Cloud 27, Heaven

Subject: Faith
From: Bartholomew Pennington <barthpenn@heaven.org>
Date: Sat, 26 July 2003 17:22:19
To: genwillow@kingdom.org

Dearest Genny,

I just left the hospital where Jordon Mink is dying. He is not expected to live but a few hours more.

I have no idea where St. Andrew is. He's probably with St. Hawthorne planning my exile from Heaven.

I am writing you from the boy's computer. I'm in his tiny bedroom. It's a room where a little boy lived who had great dreams but never believed he was good enough to succeed at anything.

Genny, do you remember passing on and arriving here? Do you recall what it was like to be a mortal? Do you recall when *faith* was the biggest word on Earth?

Faith: such a comforting, yet tormenting word. F*aith:* it's *believing* without *knowing*.

Remember what it was like *believing* in God, Genny, when all we had was our faith? Then, when we passed away and our souls came here, it was no longer a belief but true. Do you remember on Earth when we only believed in Heaven? Do you remember how we had to believe in miracles?

Here I am, sitting in a little mortal's room, where you *must* have faith in God, the Heavens, and in miracles. Here on Earth you must believe. I ask you, at this moment, what does Jordon Mink have to believe in anymore? I wonder?

Is there *no hope*?

I am returning to Cloud Nine. I do not belong here anymore. There is nothing I can do. And I suppose St. Andrew will want

---

kevin scott collier

to be seeing me very soon.

Jordon jokingly liked to address me as a "loser" in many of his letters. You know, Genny, I am willing to be a loser in Heaven, if only he can be a winner on Earth.

Sincerely,
Bart

Subject: HOPE
From: Gennif Willow <genwillow@kingdom.org>
Date: Sat, 26 July 2003 17:39:14
To: barthpenn@heaven.org

Dear Bart,

Never give up on hope, or it will give up on *you*.

All my love,
Genny

Subject: My office tomorrow
From: Andrew Wellsworth III <st.andrew@kingdom.org>
Date: Sat, 26 July 2003 17:57:26
To: barthpenn@heaven.org

Dear Bartholomew,

Effective immediately your position of Angel 2nd Order is terminated.

Daniel Hillsdale has assumed your position effective immediately.

Be here on my Cloud tomorrow morning at 7:00 sharp.

Sincerely,
St. Andrew
Administrator of Angels, 1st Order
The Kingdom of God

Subject: I apologize
From: Bartholomew Pennington <barthpenn@heaven.org>
Date: Sat, 26 July 2003 18:05:09
To: genwillow@kingdom.org

Dearest Genny,

I am to meet with St. Andrew tomorrow morning.

My position here has been terminated.

Lord *knows* the mistakes I've made around here, and I only have myself to blame.

But this time whatever may come, it was a hole worth digging.

Sincerely,
Bart

barthpenn@heaven.org

<Chapter Four>

<RESTART>

From: Jordon Mink <jordonmink@intelweb.com>
To: barthpenn@heaven.org
Sent: Sun, 27 July 2003 18:19:12
Subject: ???

BART?

From: Jordon Mink <jordonmink@intelweb.com>
To: barthpenn@heaven.org
Sent: Sun, 27 July 2003 18:24:37
Subject: ???

BART,

ARE YOU THERE?

Subject: Re: ???
From: Bartholomew Pennington <barthpenn@heaven.org>
Date: Sun, 27 July 2003 18:26:03
To: jordonmink@intelweb.com

JORDON?

From: Jordon Mink <jordonmink@intelweb.com>
To: barthpenn@heaven.org
Sent: Sun, 27 July 2003 18:37:12
Subject: Hey LOSER, guess who's back?

Hey BART,

GUESS who got out of the hospital this afternoon???

ONLY ONE GUESS PER CUSTOMER PLEASE!!!! TIME'S
UP!!!

ME, you loser!!! LOL.

I got better in ONE DAY! Can you believe that???

Doctors told Mom and Dad they had never seen anything like it.
Whatever was wrong with me disappeared. So I was OUTTA
THERE! LEAVIN' STEVEN!!! LOL.

But it's kinda scary, BART. I wasn't supposed to BE HERE
today. I was supposed to be, well, where YOU are! Not that I
don't want to ever meet you, but it's just NOT my time, Bud!

Mom and Dad said Brandon and his Mom came to the hospital
when I was VERY sick, and Brandon slept out in the lobby
Friday night and stayed most of Saturday. I didn't see him. I
don't recall much. I was told Mrs. Findley was there too!

Neighbors and friends came to be with my family, and so did my
soccer teammates, Coach Jeff, and Counselors Davis and
Beecham from Camp Broken Arrow.

I now know what Mr. Baxter meant when he wrote, "By the end
of our lives, we have become a collection of everyone who ever
loved us." He didn't mean a bunch of people would be there for
me when I died. He MEANT I have become a little piece of
everyone who touched me with love and kindness. COOL! Now,
make sure you tell Mr. Baxter that the NEXT time you bump
into him!

It's good to be home. I couldn't wait to write you!

BART, is this what you would call a miracle????

g2g ttyl,
Jordon

Subject: Miracle
From: Bartholomew Pennington <barthpenn@heaven.org>
Date: Sun, 27 July 2003 18:50:31
To: jordonmink@intelweb.com

Jordon,

Yes, this is what you would call a *miracle*.

Now, start making ripples, my little pebble.

Your friend,
Bart

From: Jordon Mink <jordonmink@intelweb.com>
To: barthpenn@heaven.org
Sent: Sun, 27 July 2003 19:05:16
Subject: Ripples?

Hey BART,

RIPPLES????
PEBBLE????
DUH!!!
Save that story, WHATEVER IT IS, for ANOTHER time. OK???

I just wanted to tell you while we're trading messages; I found the feather under my hospital pillow Saturday night. I know YOU hid it there even though you'd NEVER say so!!! This makes me think that I should HIDE my diary in a better spot or maybe even PUT A LOCK ON IT!!!!!

I put the feather back in the May 30 spot. You hafta know what that's all about. BUT you should have noticed when you were SNOOPING around in my diary that I didn't write a single word about you in there! Marking a blank page isn't telling anything. It's keeping a SECRET. A PROMISE made; a PROMISE kept!

Speaking of secrets, I know you can't tell me secrets about Heaven, but if you had anything to do with me getting better, THANK YOU!

Your friend,
Jordon

Subject: (no subject)
From: Bartholomew Pennington <barthpenn@heaven.org>
Date: Sun, 27 July 2003 19:14:40
To: jordonmink@intelweb.com

Jordon,

You're welcome.

I regret I have to tell you this but except for a final reply, I must ask you to *never* email me at this address again.

Things have changed, and I will not be here on Cloud Nine anymore.

Sincerely,
Bart

BART,

I knew this day was coming, but I'm not mad. Angels just can't talk to kids on Earth. I understand. You probably got into a lot of trouble over this.

Ever since I got a Bible to call my own, I've been curious about your kind. There are a lot of feathers in it marking spirits like you. I always prayed one day I would come to know one. And I did. I will always love you, Bartholomew, and I will miss you.

I will delete your email address now and not a trace of you will be there. But a trace of you will always be in my heart.

Bye,
Jordon

Subject: Hold on . . .
From: Bartholomew Pennington <barthpenn@heaven.org>
Date: Sun, 27 July 2003 19:33:10
To: jordonmink@intelweb.com

Jordon,

I said you could never write me at this email address again. H*owever*, you can email me at my *new* address beginning tomorrow. It is barthpenn@kingdom.org.

I've been promoted!

As always, it's *our secret.*

Sincerely,
Bartholomew Pennington
Angel, 1st Order
Assistant to St. Andrew
Cloud 99, Heaven

From: Jordon Mink <jordonmink@intelweb.com>
To: barthpenn@heaven.org
Sent: Sun, 27 July 2003 19:39:20
Subject: ???

Congratulations, LOSER!!!!

LOL.

ttyl!!!!
Jordon

Subject: Congratulations!
From: Gennif Willow <genwillow@kingdom.org>
Date: Sun, 27 July 2003 19:51:37
To: barthpenn@heaven.org
cc: barthpenn@kingdom.org

Dear Bartholomew,

Daniel Hillsdale just wrote and told me the news about your promotion. Congratulations! (Thanks for telling me first!)

I heard that your little friend on Earth has recovered rather *miraculously*. I think I have learned a new lesson about digging holes. Sometimes you find something quite precious at the bottom of one.

Sincerely,
Gennif Willow
Angel, 2nd Order, Administrative
Cloud 27, Heaven

Subject: Thank you
From: Bartholomew Pennington <barthpenn@heaven.org>
Date: Sun, 27 July 2003 20:14:35
To: st.andrew@kingdom.org

Dearest St. Andrew,

I want to thank you and St. Hawthorne for the new opportunity on Cloud 99.

I apologize for the mistakes I made over the last two months. I put you both in a difficult position. I should have been more careful when I typed that email address on May 25. Then it wouldn't have gotten into the wrong hands.

Looking forward to working with you tomorrow.

Sincerely,
Bartholomew Pennington
Angel, 1st Order
Assistant to St. Andrew
Cloud 99, Heaven

Subject: See you tomorrow
From: Andrew Wellsworth III <st.andrew@kingdom.org>
Date: Sun, 27 July 2003 20:31:52
To: barthpenn@heaven.org

Dear Bartholomew,

Concerning the email of May 25th: What makes you think it *did* get into the *wrong* hands?

St. Hawthorne and I kept a close eye on you, Brother Bartholomew. We saw the shenanigans like your "Youth Soccer Game" and sneaking the feather from Jordon's diary and hiding it under his hospital pillow. But it was the kite which became caught in the tree that made a ripple here in the Heavens. St. Hawthorne and I suspected you might rush to Earth to dislodge it. But you did not.

You asked your friend Gennif Willow what "Jordon has to believe in." We know why the kite broke free and took flight above that tree. It was because Jordon believed it would. Believing without knowing is a miraculous thing. Jordon has a lot to believe in, Bartholomew.

Bartholomew, your education here is just beginning.

Sincerely,
St. Andrew,
Administrator of Angels, 1st Order
The Kingdom of God

P.S. I enjoyed recalling your "Pebble" story. Those ripples of kindness in life can be amusing. But *who* really is the pebble? You? Me? Jordon? Mr. Baxter? Mrs. Findley? Brandon? Perhaps Bartholomew, we ALL are.

From: Karen Fischer <kfischer@intelweb.com>
To: jordonmink@intelweb.com
Sent: Sun, 27 July 2003 20:47:43
Subject: Invitation

Dear Jordon,

I am so happy you are back home and feeling better.

I was afraid I might lose my only friend, YOU. I was afraid you might have left this world without me ever being able to say, "I'm sorry."

Once you feel 100%, I would be HONORED to have YOU as a guest in my home. As you probably know by now, my Mom is raising me alone. Mom's brother Ken helps out too. Uncle Ken bought us this used computer for my schoolwork! The apartment we live in is nothing fancy. The hot water doesn't last long for showers, and we don't have cable TV.

My bedroom is NOTHING like YOURS! The best thing about my room is your eagle drawing taped on the wall!!! There are a lot of things I don't have, Jordon, but when you come here, we will have each other.

Still friends?
Brandon

From: Jordon Mink <jordonmink@intelweb.com>
To: kfischer@intelweb.com
Sent: Sun, 27 July 2003 20:59:05
Subject: FOR BRANDON – Friends!

Hey BRANDON,

I can come and stay with YOU???
AWWWWWWEEEEESOMMMMME!!!!

I will talk to my parents; they can get in touch with your Mom!

I look forward to meeting your Mom!!!

I have a book I'm going to bring along when I do come over. I want you to have it. It's about people LIKE US.

Friends forever,
Jordon

---

kevin scott collier   *151*

From: Jordon Mink <jordonmink@intelweb.com>
To: barthpenn@kingdom.org
Sent: Mon, 28 July 2003 08:33:14
Subject: Got invited over!!!

Hey, BIG SHOT,

I had to write! I've been invited over to Brandon's apartment! I will keep you posted.

And please, try to stay out of trouble on your new job. OK?

g2g ttyl,
JORDON

Subject: Big shot?
From: Bartholomew Pennington <barthpenn@kingdom.org>
Date: Mon, 28 July 2003 09:13:45
To: jordonmink@intelweb.com

Dear Jordon,

That is great news about Brandon!

I got my first big assignment already today. Actually, it's an additional title to Angel 1st Order.

Curious to know what it is?

Sincerely,
Bartholomew Pennington
Angel, 1st Order
Assistant to St. Andrew
Cloud 99, Heaven

From: Jordon Mink <jordonmink@intelweb.com>
To: barthpenn@kingdom.org
Sent: Mon, 28 July 2003 09:16:57
Subject: OK . . .

BART,

Want me to feed your ego? OK, what's the BIG NEW TITLE you have now?

Jordon

Subject: Ego?
From: Bartholomew Pennington <barthpenn@kingdom.org>
Date: Mon, 28 July 2003 09:20:21
To: jordonmink@intelweb.com

Jordon,

My boss, St. Andrew, has designated me to be your Guardian Angel.

That is, of course, if *you* approve.

Sincerely,
Bartholomew Pennington
Angel, 1st Order
Assistant to St. Andrew
Cloud 99, Heaven

From: Jordon Mink <jordonmink@intelweb.com>
To: barthpenn@kingdom.org
Sent: Mon, 28 July 2003 09:25:11
Subject: AWESOME!!!

Hey BART,

I will AGREE to accept you as my Guardian Angel under one condition.

Next time you let ME deal with POOPER Milligan!

g2g ttyl,
Jordon

Subject: LOL
From: Bartholomew Pennington <barthpenn@kingdom.org>
Date: Mon, 28 July 2003 09:29:16
To: jordonmink@intelweb.com

DEAL!

g2g ttyl,
Bart

barthpenn@heaven.org

And so it was that Bartholomew Pennington and Jordon Mink
continued their special friendship. And never once, during
Jordon's lifetime, was that secret relinquished.